"Trust me, I've had a lot of practice resisting you."

Rayanne blinked and stared up at him. "Excuse me?"

Blue was surprised that she was surprised.

"You think all that time we worked on those cases together that my mind was solely on the job? I've been attracted to you since day one."

For just a heartbeat, she looked a little pleased about that. Then she shook her head. "You don't remember all that, remember?"

"Oh, I remember some things."

Things that caused him to stray into the stupid realm again, because he brushed a kiss on her cheek. Thank goodness it was only her cheek, because he could have sworn he saw little lightning bolts zing through her eyes.

She let go of him so fast that he had no choice but to sit back on the bed or he would have fallen. Blue, this can't happen again."

He nodded. "I know."

And he did.

Didn't he?

RUSTLING UP TROUBLE

USA TODAY Bestselling Author
DELORES FOSSEN

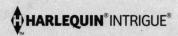

Recycling programs
for this product may
not exist in your area.

ISBN-13: 978-0-373-69794-6

Rustling Up Trouble

Copyright © 2014 by Delores Fossen

Printed in U.S.A.

ABOUT THE AUTHOR

USA TODAY bestselling author Delores Fossen has sold over fifty novels with millions of copies of her books in print worldwide. She's received the Booksellers' Best Award and the RT Reviewers' Choice Award, and was a finalist for a prestigious RITA® Award. In addition, she's had nearly a hundred short stories and articles published in national magazines. You can contact the author through her webpage at www.dfossen.net.

Books by Delores Fossen

HARLEQUIN INTRIGUE

CAST OF CHARACTERS

Agent Blue McCurdy—Five months ago he disappeared and was presumed dead. Now he's back at Sweetwater Ranch with killers on his trail, broken memories and secrets that could put everyone around him in danger.

Deputy Rayanne McKinnon—After Blue disappeared, she wrote him out of her life, but she has a secret of her own.

Rex Gandy—A career criminal who was the central figure of a Justice Department investigation right before Blue disappeared.

Caleb Wiggs—Blue's boss in the Justice Department, but he's not offering a lot of information to help fill in Blue's memories.

Woody Janson—A former agent. He'd been on the run for months, but no one knows why.

Jewell McKinnon—Rayanne's mother, who's in jail awaiting trial for murder.

Wendell Braddock—Jewell is accused of murdering his son, and he's made no secret about hating the McKinnons.

Chapter One

Deputy Rayanne McKinnon's breath stalled in her throat, and she did a double take. No, her eyes hadn't deceived her.

She was looking at a dead man.

At least, he was supposed to be dead.

But dead men didn't move, and this one was definitely doing that.

He was crouched behind a big pile of rocks. And he had his attention trained on the back fence that coiled around the pasture of her family's ranch. It was that particular fence and a tripped security sensor that'd caused Rayanne to ride out and have a look. She'd figured a cow had gotten out.

She darn sure hadn't expected to find *him*.

Even though he was a good twenty yards away and had his face partially concealed with a low-slung white Stetson, Rayanne had no trouble recognizing him.

Blue McCurdy.

Just the sight of his ink-black hair, rangy body and chiseled face sent her stomach churning. An invisible meaty fist clamped around her heart, squeezing and choking until her chest was throbbing like a toothache.

The memories came. All bad.

Well, mostly bad, anyway.

Rayanne pushed aside the ones that were good, including the little tug of relief at seeing Blue alive.

She cursed both her reaction and the man himself. Blue was the last person on God's green earth she expected or wanted to see, and yet here he was on McKinnon land.

The question was, why?

This couldn't be about the baby.

Could it?

Rayanne opened her mouth to shout out that *why* as to the alive part and remind him that he was trespassing. But a sound stopped her cold. The soft rumble of some kind of engine, and it was moving along the fence line.

Blue reached beneath his leather vest and pulled a gun from the back waist of his jeans.

That got her heart thumping, and not in a "relieved you're alive" sort of way. Rayanne drew her Colt, too, and stepped behind a live oak. As a deputy sheriff, she'd had more than her share of experience in dealing with bad guys.

Blue McCurdy included.

If he was up to something shady, and it was pretty clear that he was, then Blue had brought trouble practically to her doorstep. That was another *why,* and Rayanne hoped she got answers soon.

The engine sounds stopped, and Blue adjusted his gun. Whoever was out there had put him on edge. He certainly wasn't jumping out from those rocks to greet anyone.

Mercy.

If this was trouble worse than Blue himself, then things were going to be *bad.*

She wanted to watch for a few more seconds to try to figure out what was going on here, but just in case things went from bad to worse, she'd have to fire off a text to someone who could respond from the ranch house. There wasn't good enough phone reception in this part of the property for a call, but a text would usually go through. She'd learned that during the three months she'd been back here at Sweetwater Ranch while awaiting her mother's murder trial.

That put the clamp on her heart again, and she cursed it, too.

Blasted feelings!

Why the heck did they have to keep messing with her head and every other part of her? It had to be the pregnancy hormones, because she'd never felt this moody and whiny before.

Rayanne thankfully didn't have time to dwell on that, because she saw the movement in the trees behind the fence. Blue must have seen it, too, because he ducked lower.

Waiting.

Not hiding.

It was a subtle enough difference for Rayanne to ready her Colt. She didn't want Blue dead before he could explain to her all those *whys* that kept racking up.

Including why he'd left her naked in bed nearly five months ago.

Rayanne cursed him again and cursed herself for allowing any man to get that close to her. It wouldn't happen again, and as soon as she found out what Blue wanted, she'd send him on his way.

Or maybe arrest him.

Another flicker of movement, and this time she got a glimpse of a man dressed in dark clothes. Tall, marine-like build. Definitely not a friendly sort.

That got her tugging her phone from the back pocket of her jeans, and she sent a quick text to her stepbrother, FBI agent Seth Calder, to request some backup. Hopefully, he was still at the ranch and hadn't left for work yet, so he could get there in a hurry.

"McCurdy?" someone shouted.

But Blue didn't answer.

The shouter yelled Blue's surname again, and this time Rayanne got more than a glimpse. She saw his face and picked through the features to see if she knew him.

She didn't.

But apparently Blue knew the guy well enough to hide from him.

"We know you're here," the man added. "And we're not leaving until someone dies."

That felt like a punch to her chest. Yes, she was a cop, but that didn't mean she enjoyed diving into gunfights, especially now that she had someone else to consider.

Her unborn baby.

Plus, she wasn't exactly keen on taking a huge risk like this to save a man whom she hated.

"Damn you, Blue," she mumbled, and debated if she should identify herself. It might get the gunman running.

Or not.

It was just as likely to get him to start shooting. Because it was clear this guy wasn't a cop out to arrest Blue. Cops didn't make threats like that.

Not good cops, anyway.

She glanced back at the paint gelding that she'd ridden in on. He was grazing on some pasture grass and would maybe stay put. Rayanne didn't want him in the middle of, well, whatever the heck this was.

Keeping her gun ready, she crouched down and hurried behind another tree. Then another. Moving closer to a dry spring bed that was deep enough to give her some cover. It was also closer to Blue. When she slipped behind a third tree, Blue snapped his head in her direction.

Their eyes met.

Rayanne's narrowed.

His eyes widened.

Blue didn't seem any happier to see her than she was to see him, and using just his left hand, he made a sharp palm-down gesture that Rayanne had no trouble interpreting.

Stay put.

Something he darn sure didn't do.

She could have sworn that her presence changed whatever plan Blue had had in mind, because he appeared to curse, and then he maneuvered toward the end of the line of boulders. Away from her. And closer to the big guy who'd warned him that someone was going to die.

At the rate he was going, that someone would be Blue.

She saw the man's hand snake out. Gun clutched and aimed. He fired right into those boulders where he'd no doubt heard Blue moving around. The bullet smacked into the stone, making a sharp zinging sound, and it was quickly followed by another shot.

Another gunman, too.

No. Not this. If all Hades was going to break loose, why not wait until she had backup?

The shooter's partner ducked out from cover just a few yards from Blue and pulled the trigger. That one clipped the boulder at just the right angle to send some rock chips flying right at Blue. Rayanne got just a glimpse of the blood from the nicks those rocks caused before more shots came.

Sweet heaven. She couldn't just stand by and let this happen. Rayanne scrambled into the dry spring bed, keeping as low as she could, but she lifted her head just enough so she could take aim at the marine-sized guy.

She fired.

And missed, but it got his attention, all right.

Blue's, too.

He cursed at her. "Get down!" Blue yelled.

Rayanne had no choice but to do just that when the gunman sent a shot her way. *Too close.* Ditto for the one he aimed at Blue.

She fired back but didn't wait to see if she'd hit one of them. Then she scrambled down the spring bed, making her way to the boulders that Blue was using for cover.

"What part of *get down* didn't you understand?" Blue snarled.

No greeting, no explanation as to why he was on her family's ranch with gunmen after him.

Just that barked question.

Thankfully, his attention didn't go in the direction of her stomach, because it wasn't a good time to have to explain the small baby bump that she had hopefully hidden enough with her bulky jacket.

"I'm the one with a badge," Rayanne snarled back. "So if anyone should be staying down, it's you. Plus, you lost your right to give me any kind of advice when you disappeared without so much as a word."

Yeah, the timing for those words sucked, but Rayanne couldn't stop herself. Blue had crushed her, and it was hard to fight back all those emotions.

"You want to save your girl, McCurdy?" the man yelled. "Then both of you put down your guns and come with us so we can talk."

Rayanne clamped her hand over Blue's arm in case he intended to fall for that. Clearly these fools didn't have talking in mind. But Blue didn't move. He only glanced down at where she had hold of him. His long-sleeve black shirt was between her hand and his skin, but she could have sworn she felt every inch of him.

Every inch.

And she cursed her body's reaction again, along with jerking back her hand. Definitely not the time for those memories to rear their ugly, hot little heads.

"Time's up, McCurdy," the man added. "Come out now or you die."

The last word of that threat had barely left his mouth when the shots started again. This time it was Blue who did the clamping. He took her by the shoulder and pushed her to the ground. Her mouth landed right in the dirt and blades of grass that hadn't already been stomped down.

Rayanne didn't stay down, though. She wasn't sure why Blue was suddenly playing cowboy-in-shining-armor, but she wasn't having any part of it.

"Please tell me these bad guys are really bad," she said, levering herself up just enough to get off a shot. "Bad as in worse than you and that this isn't some botched attempt to arrest you."

His gaze cut to her, and those gunmetal-blue eyes narrowed. "No one's as bad as I am."

He paused as if waiting for her to agree or disagree. She didn't do either, but a comment like that definitely fell into the agreement category. Of course, she'd known Blue was a bad boy before she landed in bed with him, so it shouldn't have surprised her that he'd continued his bad-boy ways.

"If you're asking if they're the law," he added, "they aren't."

Rayanne almost pressed him for more about why they were after him, but it'd have to wait. The directions of the shots changed, and it wasn't a good change, either. The two gunmen appeared to be moving away from each other and closing in on Blue and her.

Blue glanced at her again. "You take the one on the right. I'll get the one on the left."

Just on principle, she hated taking orders from Blue, but it was a decent plan considering their position. Rayanne waited, listened, and when she thought she had a good pinpoint on the shooter, she leaned out and fired. Beside her, Blue did the same.

Rayanne heard the two sounds almost simultaneously. The thud of the bullet and a groan of pain. But it wasn't her shot that'd caused those sounds.

It was Blue's.

He'd hit his target, but judging from the way the bullets kept coming, she'd missed hers.

The man who'd done all the shouting started to curse, and she tried to follow the sound of his ripe profanity. It was hard to tell where he was as he darted through the woods toward his partner, who was either injured or dead. Rayanne was hoping it was the latter because she didn't want to battle a riled, injured would-be killer.

She leaned out from the rocks again, aiming her gun at the sound of the movement and the footsteps. But another shot came their way.

Mercy.

Not from one of the two gunmen but from another direction. To their far left.

Rayanne pivoted toward the newcomer and fired. This

time she didn't miss, but again she couldn't tell if the man was just injured or dead, because the shots from the other gunmen drowned out any telltale sounds.

But there was no mistaking one sound.

Even over the blasts and her own heartbeat crashing in her ears, she heard—and felt—one of those bullets. It didn't slam into her.

It hit Blue.

And it didn't just hit him. It tore off a chunk of rock that smacked against his left temple. She knew the exact second of impact from both the bullet and the rock. Blue groaned in pain.

And Rayanne could only watch as he collapsed against her.

She didn't look at him. Was too afraid of what she might see. Besides, she had to deal with the person who'd fired that shot.

The anger slammed into her, along with the fear she had for the baby. She tried to shut out all thoughts when she took aim. However, she didn't get a chance to fire. That was because the moron stopped shooting and started running.

Escaping.

Rayanne nearly bolted after him, but then she looked down at Blue. Unconscious. He was breathing, sucking in shallow breaths, and there wasn't a drop of color in Blue's face.

But there was color everywhere else. Lots of it.

From his blood spilling onto her.

Chapter Two

Blue heard the voices and opened his eyes.

Big mistake. The light stabbed through his head like razors, and a very unmanly sounding groan clawed its way through his parched throat.

That stopped the voices.

He heard movement. People shuffling around, and despite the pain, he reached for his gun.

Not there.

Even though it was hard to think, he figured this couldn't be good. Unarmed and in god-awful pain. He hoped he didn't have to fight his way out of there, because judging from the way he felt, he'd already had his butt kicked bad.

Blue had another go at opening his eyes. This time he took things slower and cracked just one eyelid so he could have a look. There was an elderly man with salt-and-pepper hair looming over him. No gun, either, but he was sporting a very concerned expression.

"I'm Dr. Wilbert Howland," the man said. "I did your surgery."

It took Blue a moment to process that. Surgery likely meant a hospital, so he glanced around.

Yep.

He was in bed, flat on his back, surrounded by sterile white walls and an antiseptic smell.

"Surgery?" Blue repeated. He tried to pick through the images and sounds that spun like an F5 tornado through his head.

"You were shot," the doctor provided. "And you have a concussion."

With the help of the ache in his left shoulder nudging him, Blue remembered getting shot and being smacked in the head with a piece of flying rock. Hard to forget the blistering pain from those two things. He also remembered the gunmen.

Three of them.

That gave him a jolt of concern. "Where are the guys who shot me?"

"Two are dead. The other one's missing."

Blue groaned again. "The missing one will come for me." At least Blue thought he would.

"You're safe here. And you're going to be fine," the doc assured him. "The bullet didn't hit anything vital, but you did lose a lot of blood because it took a while to get an ambulance out there to you."

No memory of an ambulance. Zero. No memory of how much time had passed, either. Definitely something he should be able to recall.

"Where are my clothes?" he asked, glancing down at the hospital gown.

"Bagged. I'll have someone bring them to you if the sheriff doesn't need them for processing."

Right. Because the clothes might be needed for an investigation. "I want the Stetson and the vest. They're my good-luck charms," he added.

The doc gave him a funny look. No doubt because he was in the hospital. But he was also alive.

That meant the good-luck charms had worked again.

The doctor leaned closer and waved a little penlight in front of Blue's eyes. More pain. Heck, breathing made it worse, too.

"If it hadn't been for Rayanne," the doctor said, "you might have bled out. She added pressure to your wound to slow down the blood flow."

"Rayanne," Blue managed to say, and he got a glimpse of her peering over the doctor's shoulder.

The relief was instant, and Blue released the breath he didn't even know he'd been holding.

Yeah, it was her, all right.

She had her ginger-brown hair pulled into her usual ponytail, though strands had slipped out and were dangling around her face and shoulders. When she stepped to the doctor's side, he saw the blood on the front of her buckskin-colored jacket.

"You're hurt." Blue tried to sit up, but the doctor stopped that.

Rayanne shook her head. "That's not my blood. It's yours."

More relief. It was bad enough that he'd been shot, but it would have been much worse if the bullet had gone into Rayanne instead.

But why did she look so, well, riled at him?

This wasn't the first time they'd gotten shot at together. As an ATF agent, he had worked on a few cases with her when the investigations had landed in her jurisdiction. So why was she eyeing him now as if she wanted to rip off his aching head?

And the questions just kept coming.

Why had he been shot, and where the heck was he? He knew the hospital part, but he'd been in several hospitals in San Antonio, his hometown, and this wasn't one of them.

"Why'd those men want you dead?" Rayanne asked. "Why aren't *you* dead?" she tacked onto that.

Clearly she had some questions of her own.

Blue opened his mouth to get busy answering them and realized he didn't have a clue. "Start from the beginning," he insisted. "I want to know what's going on. Why can't I remember how I got here?"

Rayanne huffed. More eye narrowing, and those gray eyes that at times could take on a warm, sensual glow certainly weren't warm or sensual at the moment. They were like little slabs of ice jabbing at him.

"A sensor alarm went off at the ranch," she finally said, "and when I rode out to check, I found you trying not to draw the attention of three gunmen who drove up on the back side of the fence."

On one level that gave him a serious shot of adrenaline, but on another it was just plain confusing.

Think, Blue.

Not easy to do, but he sorted through some of the fog and remembered going to the ranch that Rayanne's family owned.

Estranged family, he mentally corrected.

Rayanne had told him that she might have to go back to Sweetwater Springs because her mother was possibly going to be arrested for the decades-old murder of an alleged lover, Whitt Braddock.

And that was where Blue's memories came to a grinding halt.

"Why were the gunmen there?" he asked. "And why are you so mad?"

Her next huff was considerably louder. "Could you give us a minute?" Rayanne asked the doc.

Dr. Howland didn't seem exactly comfortable with that, but he eventually nodded. "Only for a minute or two. And go easy on him."

"You want to know why I'm mad?" Rayanne repeated once the doctor had stepped out. "Well, for starters you slept with me almost five months ago and then disappeared without so much as a Post-it note."

Oh, man.

He'd slept with her?

Blue remembered the attraction between them. Felt it blood-deep even now. But he'd always fought falling into bed with her because he had a strict rule about not having sex with coworkers.

Blue shook his head. "I don't remember."

And that was saying something. Rayanne wasn't exactly forgettable, and sex with her should have stuck in his mind like permanent glue.

"I have amnesia?" he asked. That was sadly the best-case scenario here. The worst would be some kind of permanent brain damage.

She lifted her shoulder. "You'd have to ask the doctor about that."

And he would, the second the man came back. For now, though, he needed as much info as possible. "What happened after I disappeared?"

Rayanne studied him, the way a cop would study a suspect she thought was lying through his teeth. "I got word that you were dead. I can't think of any good reason you'd let me believe that other than you really did want me out of your life."

Oh, mercy.

It felt as if twin heavyweights had slugged each side of his jaw at the same time. Blue couldn't speak. Heck, he couldn't even catch his breath. Yeah, he was pretty much the love-'em-and-leave-'em sort, but there was no way he'd do something like that to Rayanne.

Would he?

"I looked for you when you left," she continued, "but I got a message from your foster brother saying you were dead. That you'd been killed in Mexico."

There was a massive amount of fog in his head, but he could sort through enough to remember some things.

"I don't have a brother, either a real one or a foster," he insisted. "And I sure as hell didn't die in Mexico. I'm right here." Blue reached for her, but she stepped back as if he'd tried to tase her.

Before Blue could get out of bed and do something to convince her that he wasn't the bad guy here, the door flew open. Blue reached for his gun again. Cursed when it wasn't where it belonged.

However, Rayanne pulled her Colt from her shoulder holster.

False alarm. It was Dr. Howland, but he wasn't alone.

The sandy-haired, linebacker-sized guy who came through the door spared her and then her gun a glance as he flashed his badge and made a beeline for Blue. Thankfully, this man wasn't a blurry memory.

It was Blue's boss, Agent Caleb Wiggs, from the Bureau of Alcohol, Tobacco, Firearms and Explosives—ATF.

At least, Caleb had been his boss five months ago.

With everything else going on, Blue figured he could be wrong about that, too.

Rayanne seemed to know him, as well, and judging from her scowl, Caleb wasn't on her list of friends, either. She reholstered the Colt as if she'd declared war on it, but she watched him with those cop's eyes.

"You all right, Blue?" Caleb asked. He set a bag on the foot of the bed.

No way could Blue answer yes to that question. It might garner him a lightning bolt for such a big lie. "What's going on?"

Caleb didn't answer, but he looked at Rayanne and the doctor. "I need to talk to Agent McCurdy in private."

"Agent McCurdy?" Rayanne questioned. She huffed. "Don't you mean *former* agent?"

That got Blue's complete attention. Great day in the morning. Along with his mind and gun, had he managed to lose his badge, too?

"I mean *agent*." And Caleb didn't sound any friendlier than Rayanne. "Blue still works for me."

"Wait a minute," Blue said, trying to figure this out. It didn't help that his shoulder started clamoring for more pain meds. "What's the date?"

"October 6," the doctor provided. "And I hope everyone remembers that I just dug a bullet out of my patient here. He needs some peace and quiet so he can recover."

"And he'll get it," Caleb insisted. "I've already made arrangements to have him moved." He tipped his head to the bag. "Figured you could use a change of clothes for the drive to another hospital. One where I can make sure you have some security."

"He's not going anywhere, not until I get some answers first," Rayanne insisted right back.

That started a staring match between his boss and the deputy he'd apparently crossed lines with. Big ones.

All four of them volleyed glances at each other. "I'll give you a few more minutes," the doctor finally said. "After that my patient *will* get some rest."

Dr. Howland shot Caleb and Rayanne a warning glance that only an experienced doctor in charge could have managed, and he walked out.

Even with the doc's latest exit, Caleb didn't answer right away, and when he finally did open his mouth, he looked at Rayanne, not Blue.

"I can't wrap all of this up in a neat little package for you," Caleb started. "I honestly don't know why Blue disappeared."

"You said it was because he had ties to criminals," Rayanne reminded him.

Oh, man. And Blue just kept mentally repeating that.

"He did have criminal ties." Caleb's gaze finally came to Blue's. "If you've got an explanation about that, I'd like to hear it, because you didn't just disappear five months ago. You walked away from your job at the Justice Department, and the only reason you're still on payroll is because I've covered your butt and put you on a leave of absence."

Hell. This just kept getting worse. Not the leave-of-absence part but the reason Caleb had been forced to do something like that for him.

Criminal ties?

No way. He didn't need his memory to know that.

"The doc must have given me some meds that messed with my head." A head that Blue now shook. "Because the last thing I remember was finishing up a case with Rayanne. After that, it's just bits and pieces that don't make sense. Why did I leave? And why did I come to the McKinnon ranch today with gunmen after me?"

"That's what I'd like to know," Rayanne mumbled, but then she waved off any answer he might give. "My brother Seth got IDs on the two dead guys. The bodies are being examined now, and there's a CSI team searching the woods for evidence."

Seth, an FBI agent. Blue had never met him, but he'd heard Rayanne mention him.

"The dead men's names are Leland Chadwell and Brian Kipp," Rayanne continued, and she watched his face. Maybe to see if there was any sign of recognition.

There wasn't.

Blue had to shake his head again. "Who are they?"

"They're hired thugs," Caleb provided, "and, among other criminal sorts, they often work for Rex Gandy."

Now, that was a name that rang bells the size of Texas.

Could this mess possibly get any crazier?

Gandy wasn't just a thug—he was a rich one and had all kinds of nasty ties to gunrunners, money launderers and drug traffickers. As an ATF agent, Blue had dealt with Gandy on several occasions but always when he'd been undercover, and Blue had never been able to find evidence to arrest the piece of dirt.

"Gandy hired these men to come after me," Blue said like gospel. "Why?"

Caleb gave him an odd look, as if the question had come out of left field. "You don't know?"

Since it seemed the answer was clear to both Caleb and Rayanne, Blue went with the obvious answer. "Because Gandy's riled that I keep investigating him." But he investigated a lot of people, and that didn't spur an attack to kill. "Why come after me now?"

Again, he got that look. Obviously, he was missing something here.

"I've arranged to have Gandy brought in for an interview," Caleb added.

That was a good start, but Blue wanted a whole lot more. "You plan to answer my question about why Gandy would want me dead now?"

Caleb shrugged. "I figure it's connected to whatever the heck you've been doing for the past five months, and I don't have any details about that." He mumbled something that Blue didn't catch and scrubbed his hand over the back of his neck. "I need to talk to Dr. Howland and see how long this memory problem of yours is going to last."

Caleb added some really bad profanity and made a swift exit. Only then did Blue see the cop outside his door. Local, no uniform, but he had a badge clipped to his belt and was wearing a sidearm.

That didn't do much to ease the already twisted knot in Blue's gut.

Of course, a cop-bodyguard was only partially responsible for that. The main reason for the knot was the woman standing beside his bed and glaring at him.

"All of this is true?" he came out and asked.

She nodded. Her jaw muscles stirred. And she studied him. "Is this memory thing an act?"

"No." He couldn't say it fast enough. "I have no reason to fake memory loss."

He hoped.

Though he knew it would hurt, Blue lifted his head off the pillow and levered himself up. It wasn't pretty, and he did a lot of wobbling to get to a sitting position.

"What the heck do you think you're doing?" Rayanne snarled, and she reached out to take him by the arms.

Probably to force him back down. But being flat on his back wasn't much of a bargaining position, and if he hoped to get answers from her and not smart-mouthed comebacks, he needed to try to soothe some things with Rayanne.

If that was possible.

She continued to protest, even called him a bad name, but Blue got his feet off the bed. He also reached for the metal pole that held his IV so he could use it for support.

That, however, ended a lot faster than he'd planned.

Everything started to spin, and the dark spots winking in and out prevented him from seeing much. Or keeping his balance. He would have pitched forward if Rayanne hadn't caught him.

"Don't make this worse than it already is," Rayanne snapped.

She put her hand on his back to steady him. Bare skin on bare skin.

The hospital gown hardly qualified as a garment with one side completely off his bandaged shoulder. Judging from the drafts he felt on various parts of his body, Rayanne probably got an eyeful.

Of course, it apparently wasn't something she hadn't already seen, since according to her they'd slept together five months ago.

"Will saying I'm sorry help?" he mumbled, and because he had no choice, he ditched the bargaining-position idea and lay back down.

"Nothing will help. As soon as you're back on your feet, I want you out of Sweetwater Springs and miles and miles away from McKinnon land. Got that?"

Oh, yeah. It was crystal clear.

It didn't matter that he didn't know why he'd done the things he had, but he'd screwed up. Maybe soon Blue would remember everything that he might be trying to forget.

Her phone rang, the sound shooting through the room. And his head. Rayanne fished the phone from her pocket, looked at the screen and then moved to the other side of the room to take the call. It occurred to him then that she might be involved with someone.

Five months was a long time.

And this someone might be calling to make sure she was okay.

Blue felt the twinge of jealousy that throbbed right along with the pain in various parts of his body, and he wished he could just wake up from this crazy nightmare that he was having.

"No, he doesn't remember," she said to whoever had called. She turned to look back at him, but her coat shifted to the side.

Just enough for Blue to see the stomach bulge beneath her clothes.

Oh, man.

It felt as if someone had sucked the air right out of his lungs. He didn't need his memory to understand what that meant.

Rayanne was pregnant.

Chapter Three

Rayanne heard the low groan that Blue made, and she whirled around, expecting to see some evidence that the pain had gotten significantly worse.

It wasn't pain, though, that made him groan.

His mouth was partly open, his attention fastened to her stomach, and she knew the reason for his reaction. He'd clearly noticed that she was pregnant.

Now it was her turn to groan. She hadn't intended for him to see the bump and had thought it was hidden well enough. Apparently not. It was getting harder and harder to hide it these days.

"Hold on a sec," she said to her brother Seth, who was waiting on the other end of the line with what no doubt was important info.

Probably not as important as this, though.

"Is that my baby?" Blue came right out and asked.

He'd put one and one together pretty darn fast for a man with supposed memory issues and a concussion.

Rayanne considered lying, only because she didn't want to deal with the truth right now, but if there was any trace of the real Blue left in his banged-up head, he wouldn't let go of this.

Plus, she was fed up with this whole lying mess from

Blue. It'd be like the pot calling the kettle black if she started telling whoppers, too.

"Yes, the baby's yours," she said, holding her hand over the phone so Seth couldn't hear.

Her brother already knew, of course, but she hadn't shared the news with a lot of people, only her doctor, mother and siblings. Not the estranged ones, either: Cooper, Colt and Tucker. Nor her *father,* Roy. Though she was certain that they, too, had noticed her growing belly.

Blue didn't exactly take the news well. He sucked in a quick breath, nearly choking on it. Rayanne wanted to blast him for his reaction, but the truth was, she'd been stunned, as well, when she'd seen that little plus sign on the home pregnancy test. She'd done her own share of quick breaths and head shakes.

"For the record, this is my baby, and you just happened to be the one who fathered it." She might have added more of a warning, something along the lines that Blue had zero claim to this child or any other part of her life, but she heard Seth calling out to her from over the phone.

"Can this wait a second?" Rayanne snarled to her brother.

"No," Seth snarled right back. "I'm sending you a photo of something you need to see. And this isn't a suggestion—it's an order. Stay away from McCurdy. His boss is on the way there."

With that, he hung up before she could tell him that Blue's boss had already arrived. The quick hang-up also left her to wonder what the heck else had gone wrong now.

"When are you due?" Blue asked.

Rayanne hated to give him any details whatsoever, but

it seemed a little petty to withhold something he would figure out, anyway. "In four months."

Exactly nine months to the day since Blue and she had lost their minds and landed in bed. A big mistake, obviously one he hadn't been able to handle, because he'd walked out on her—literally. She'd woken up to find him gone. No note on her pillow. No phone calls. No contact of any kind.

Until now, that is.

"Four months," he repeated, sounding like a man on the verge of losing it.

She ignored him for the time being when there was a little dinging sound from her phone to indicate she had a text. Rayanne looked at it.

And looked again.

Her shoulders tightened even more, and she stared at the liar in the bed.

"What kind of sick game are you playing, huh?" she demanded from Blue.

"No game," he assured her. "What's going on? What's got you so upset now?"

"*This* has got me upset." She shoved the phone right in his face, but judging from the way he squinted, his eyes were still too blurry to see the small print.

"Why, Blue?" she practically yelled.

It was loud enough to get the doctor and Caleb running back into the room, but Rayanne didn't budge even when Caleb tried to push her out of the way.

"He owes me an answer," Rayanne said through clenched teeth, and she showed the text to Caleb.

"Where'd you find that?" Caleb asked.

She kept her glare on Blue. "It was in his shirt pocket. The one that the medics cut off him when they put him in the ambulance. They gave it to Seth so he could process it for possible evidence."

"What is it?" Blue demanded.

"It's a hit order," Caleb finally said. Rayanne was glad he'd answered the question, because she might have choked on the words.

Blue shook his head. "Who was supposed to die?"

Rayanne's glare got worse. "Me."

She let that hang in the air for several long moments. "And the reason you were at the ranch today was because someone hired *you* to kill me."

"Not a chance. I wouldn't have agreed to do a hit on you," Blue insisted. His intense gaze swung to Caleb. "What do you know about this?"

Caleb lifted his hands, huffed. "Nothing. But then, you've been off the radar for five months, remember? I have no idea what you've been working on or who you've been working with."

And that said it all.

Maybe this was some kind of unauthorized undercover work, but it didn't matter. Whatever Blue had gotten involved in, he'd brought the danger to her and the baby. Her family, too, since her sister, brothers and father were all living on the grounds of the ranch.

The doctor checked the clock on the wall. "Those couple of minutes have long been up. Mr. McCurdy just had a bullet dug out of him and lost too much blood. He needs rest."

"I don't want to rest." Blue sat up again. Tried to stand again, too, but this time it was Caleb who stopped him. "I want to find out what's going on."

"I'll do that." Caleb's voice didn't exactly soften, but he helped Blue back onto the bed.

Not lying down.

Blue would have no part of that. Instead he sat on the edge of the mattress. "You really think I'd try to kill you?" Blue asked her.

Rayanne could feel the veins start to pulse in her head. "I don't know what to think when it comes to you."

It was impossible to keep the emotion out of that little outburst. The anger. The worry. And yes, the embarrassment. She wasn't the sort of woman who dropped into bed with a man. Any man. But especially a work partner.

Yet she had.

Once and only once had she broken that rule and slept with Blue.

And look where that'd gotten her.

Nearly killed, pregnant and she had a coat smeared with her ex-lover's blood. An ex who couldn't remember diddly-squat, including the little fact that he could have fathered her child.

However, Blue apparently did remember how to be pissed off, because his nostrils flared. "I wouldn't have killed you," he repeated.

His voice was no longer weak. Those words had a bite to them. Maybe because she'd insulted him with the accusation.

Tough.

Because it could be more than an accusation. It could be the truth.

"Then why'd you have the hit order?" she pressed.

"Those minutes are over," Dr. Howland growled.

They all ignored him, but Blue shook his head, looked at the doctor. "How long before my brain gets straight?"

"Probably a lot longer if you don't get the rest you need." He huffed. "Look, I don't know if the memory loss is from the concussion, the bleeding or the emotional trauma of being in the middle of a gunfight. The only thing I know is that most people make a complete recovery. But they do that by resting and recuperating, not by getting in a shouting match with visitors who shouldn't even be here."

"It wouldn't be from emotional trauma," Caleb volunteered, once again ignoring the doctor. "Blue's been in the middle of plenty of gunfights." He, too, checked the time. "I'll make some calls and speed up the arrangements to get you out of here."

"Is moving him a good idea?" Rayanne asked, bringing their attention back to her. It probably sounded as if she was concerned about his health.

Okay, she was.

But not in a "welcome home, lover" kind of way. She didn't want a move to delay the return of those memories, because she had to know what the devil was going on.

Dr. Howland opened his mouth to speak, but Caleb beat him to the punch. "I'm moving him. Blue's a federal agent, and he needs to be debriefed."

That got her attention fast. "Debriefed about what?" Because that was one of those fancy fed words that usually meant an agent was involved in something classified or deep undercover.

Caleb shot her a glare that could have withered spring grass. "This isn't your concern, Rayanne."

"To heck it's not." She lifted her phone screen in case he'd forgotten what was on there. "Someone hired him to kill me."

"And we'll get to the bottom of this. Not you. *We,*" Caleb repeated, tapping the shiny gold ATF badge on his belt. "I'll be back to move him," he added to no one in particular, and he left the room again.

"Your turn to leave," the doctor insisted, looking directly at her.

Rayanne started to do just that. After all, she could do her own investigating from the Sweetwater Springs sheriff's office. She wasn't a deputy there. Her job was one county over, where she was on a leave of absence. But since her brother Cooper was the sheriff and since the shooting had happened on the ranch, she figured Cooper would be more than willing to give her some space to work.

Because something beyond the obvious wasn't right here.

"I need to speak to Rayanne alone," Blue said.

She combed through every bit of his expression but couldn't tell if he was remembering something or if this was yet some other ploy. It didn't matter. If he had anything to tell her, she wanted to hear it. Because if he did indeed confess to being a hit man, she was going to arrest his butt. And she didn't care if this was a federal case or not.

Of course, if he confessed to something like that, jurisdiction was the least of her worries.

The doctor released a long, slow breath. "At least stay in bed when you talk," he demanded.

Dr. Howland added a warning glance to both of them and then went into the hall. Caleb was out there, his phone pressed to his ear. No doubt making those arrangements to move Blue to another hospital.

The moment the doctor shut the door, Blue got up again, and this time it was a slightly less wobbly attempt.

He took hold of the IV pole with his right hand and started walking.

"Don't," he mumbled as if he expected her to object.

She didn't. But Rayanne did drop back a step when those wobbly steps brought him her way. And not just her way but directly in front of her. She resisted the urge to back up some more and held her ground. No gaze dodging. No fidgeting. She put on her lawman's face and watched as he did the same.

For a second or two, anyway.

"I need to do something," he said.

That was all the warning she got before he reached out, slid his hand around the back of her neck and put his mouth on hers.

Rayanne gasped, but the sound got trapped between their lips, and Blue ignored it. He kept on kissing her. Kept on moving his mouth over hers as if he had a right to do that.

Just kept on stirring heat that should have been stone cold.

It wasn't.

And that riled her to the core.

Damn him for bringing all the heat and the memories flooding back. She'd buried Blue five months ago. Not just him, either, but that one hot night they'd shared. Rayanne intended for that to stay dead and buried.

She would have knocked him senseless, but apparently he already was. She didn't shove him away, not with all his injuries, but Rayanne slapped her palm on his stomach and then backed up.

"What the heck are you doing?" she snapped. And thank goodness it sounded gruff and not breathless.

Somewhat of a miracle since her breath was indeed a little thin.

"Still think I'd try to kill you?" Blue asked.

The cocky voice had returned in spades. Cocky demeanor, too. Blue was a pro at that in part because of his hot cowboy looks. Sadly, he was the best-looking man she'd ever met, and her stupid body wasn't going to let her forget that.

Rayanne managed to hang on to her glare. "You kissed me to convince me that you don't want me dead?"

He lifted his shoulder. The one that'd been shot. And he winced enough to wipe that cocky look off his face. "In part. I was hoping it'd make me remember."

"Did it?"

That prompted him to run those sizzling gray eyes over her face and then lower. To her breasts. Then lower still. She didn't know how he managed it, but a once-over like that from Blue felt like foreplay despite her pregnant belly.

"No," he finally said. "But trust me, I'm pretty sure every part of me but my brain remembers you."

Oh.

That felt like foreplay, too, and since that was the last thing she wanted, she did step back. She'd already had a big dose of Blue, and she wasn't sure she could survive another round with him.

Best to think about the other mess. The one that involved those gunmen, living and dead. "Why'd the shooting happen? Give me something to go on. *Anything* to go on," she added when he just stared at her.

Blue kept staring. "The last solid memory I have is the evening when we finished up that case over in Appaloosa Pass."

She knew exactly which evening he meant. Rayanne had gone over the detail dozens of times. "The investigation had gone wrong. An innocent bystander was killed."

He studied her. "We were upset."

Oh, yeah. Rayanne had never broken down before. Not in front of anyone, anyway. But she had that night, and she'd ended up in Blue's arms.

And with him in her bed.

He cleared his throat as if he'd filled in the blanks of his memory with some spicy details. "Afterward, did I say anything?" Blue asked. "Call anyone?"

"No, but someone called you. You said it was your good friend and fellow agent Woody Janson. You didn't put the call on speaker, but I heard him say he wanted you to meet him in a diner in San Antonio." Rayanne paused. "The guy sounded like he was in some kind of trouble."

His head snapped up. "So Woody might know what happened. I need to call him." Blue was already moving toward the landline on the metal table next to his bed, but Rayanne snagged his wrist to stop him.

"Woody's missing," she explained. "He has been since you left. I searched for him, but I stopped when your foster brother called to tell me you were dead. Or according to you, the man pretending to be your foster brother."

"He was definitely pretending. I'm an only child, and I had no siblings when I was placed in foster care. Did you run the number of the caller?"

She had to shake her head. Rayanne had no intention of telling him that she'd kind of fallen apart after hearing he was dead. Investigating the caller had been the last thing on her mind.

It wasn't now.

Once she had this other issue of the hit resolved, she'd

look into a fake foster brother making an equally fake death notification.

She made the mistake of looking at Blue. Her eyes meeting his. And that punch came, one that brought the memories flooding back again. For a few bad seconds, anyway. Thankfully, her phone rang, giving her mind something better to do than remember intimate things she should forget.

"Seth," she answered after seeing her stepbrother's name on the screen. "I need some good news."

"Sorry. Won't get it from me. How's Blue?" But it sounded more like something he should say rather than something he wanted to know. It was one of the reasons she loved Seth. He wasn't a natural-born hugger, but if he thought it'd help her, he'd do hugs.

And walk through fire for her.

"Blue's alive," he said, obviously able to hear Seth's question. Blue grumbled something else that she didn't catch, and he shuffled his way back to the bed, dragging the IV pole along with him.

The back of his gown was wide open, giving her a much-too-good view of his naked butt, which on a scale of one to ten was a forty-six. Rayanne did some grumbling of her own and looked away.

"What's the not-so-good news, then?" Rayanne asked Seth.

"Just got off the phone with Rex Gandy. And no, he didn't confess to hiring those gunmen who attacked Blue and you. In fact, he claims he hasn't seen them in months."

That seemed to be going around. "Please tell me you're still bringing him in for questioning."

"Yes and no. Gandy will be coming in, but I can't question him. The ATF has called dibs on this."

Rayanne tried not to groan too loud. She hadn't expected to be allowed to do the questioning, but she'd wanted Seth in on the interview. Or a second choice would have been her brother Cooper. They weren't exactly on the same side when it came to their mother's trial, but Cooper was a decent sheriff. And better yet, both Seth and he would have told her exactly what Gandy had or hadn't said.

But the ATF was a different matter.

"I'm guessing Caleb Wiggs will run the interview?" she asked.

"I'm sure he'd like that, but Gandy's already objecting."

"Why? They have some kind of history together?"

"Gandy won't say. He just told me I'd be a bloomin' fool to trust Caleb. And before you ask me, I'm already on it. I'll check out the connection between the two men and see if there's any reason for me not to trust a fellow Justice Department agent."

Good. Because she'd already been blindsided enough and didn't want to go another round with a man she couldn't trust. "If you can, go ahead and run another check on Blue's missing friend, Woody Janson."

Seth stayed quiet a moment. "You think he has something to do with this?"

"I don't know what to think," Rayanne admitted.

She heard Seth's heavy sigh. "Does Blue know about the baby?"

"He knows."

"And what the heck is he going to do about it?" Seth snapped.

"Absolutely nothing, because I'm not going to let him do anything."

Again, it seemed as if Blue had filled in the blanks about the conversation, because he glared at her in a stubborn way that only he and a mule could have managed.

"Hold a sec," Seth suddenly said, and the line went silent. Probably because he'd had to take another call.

Maybe one that would give them good news.

Any news, she amended.

She watched as Blue fumbled to get back in the bed. Another view of his backside. But it didn't hold her attention, because she saw the sweat pop out on his forehead, and he was clenching his teeth.

Clearly in pain.

Rayanne reached for the door to see if Doc Howland was still hanging around so he could give Blue another dose of meds. But reaching for the door was as far as she got.

"We have a problem," Seth blurted out when he came back on the line. "You have your gun?"

That didn't help steady her nerves, and they were already on edge just hearing the tone of Seth's voice.

"Yes. Why?" Rayanne asked her brother.

"Because I just got a call. A guy matching the description of the missing gunman was spotted on the traffic camera just a block from the hospital. He's not alone, and he's headed your way."

Chapter Four

Before Rayanne even said a word, Blue knew something else had gone wrong.

He didn't waste his energy on another groan or more profanity. He'd already been doing way too much of that, and he was already figuring this wasn't something a groan or cursing could fix.

"The guy who tried to kill you is less than a block away from the parking lot," she explained, helping him from the bed. "Backup's on the way, but it might not get here in time."

Yeah, he'd been right about that something gone wrong.

What he needed was a gun so he could try to protect Rayanne. And the baby. Of course, she wouldn't exactly appreciate any efforts from him to protect her, but she was going to get those efforts whether she wanted them or not.

Well, maybe.

His third attempt to stand wasn't any easier than his first two had been. Blue had to fight to push away the pain, but he finally got to his feet. In the same motion, he yanked the IV needle from his arm.

"What do you think you're doing?" Rayanne snarled.

"We're getting out of here. I figured that was pretty obvious."

Judging from the way her eyes widened, then narrowed, that wasn't so obvious after all, and it clearly wasn't the solution she'd had in mind. "We can hide in the bathroom."

"Bullets can go through the door, and I'd rather not be trapped in a small room with someone gunning for me."

Even if he couldn't remember who exactly wanted him dead or why. But he seriously doubted these thugs were coming here to fill in his memory gaps or have a conversation with him. Whatever he'd done to rile them, it was serious enough for them to send out a death squad. A squad that, according to the hit order, he was supposedly a part of.

He wasn't.

He hoped.

Even without the memories to prove it, Blue knew in his gut there was no way he would kill Rayanne. Agreeing to do it and making someone else believe it, however, was a different story. He could have done that for some reason that he hoped like the devil would become clear to him soon.

"My brother will be here in a few minutes," she reminded him. "And there's a deputy outside."

That was a start, but it wasn't nearly enough to fight off hired guns. "Stay away from the door," Blue warned Rayanne when she headed in that direction.

Blue rifled through the bag that Caleb had brought him, and he located some jeans, a shirt and boots. No badge or gun. But he did drag on the clothes so he could ditch the drafty gown. Every move he made was a painful effort.

"You got a backup weapon?" he asked, stepping in front of her.

A gesture that caused her to scowl and mumble something that didn't sound pleasant. "No. I only carry backup when I'm on the job."

Not good. But at least he had her weapon. Something he would have to convince her to hand over to him. Of course, that was only part of the convincing he'd have to do.

"You took a huge risk saving me earlier," he reminded her, dropping his gaze to her stomach, "and I won't let you take another one."

"It wasn't a risk."

But she stopped, knowing that there was no way she could convince him otherwise. Heck, she could no doubt still hear the sounds of the bullets flying around her. Yeah, it'd been a huge risk.

"I had no idea three gunmen would be out there when I rode out to the pasture," she added, "and I certainly didn't take the risk for you. I took it because I wasn't in a position to do anything else. If I'd tried to get out of there, one of them would have spotted me and tried to gun me down."

Fair enough. Too bad the fairness couldn't continue, because Blue snatched her gun, and before the protesting gasp could even leave her mouth, he eased open the door. The lanky dark-haired deputy was indeed still there, and he was on the phone.

"I'm Deputy Reed Caldwell," he said, his gaze snapping toward them. He shoved the phone back in his pocket. "There are three of them, and they're in the parking lot."

Man, they had gotten there even faster than he'd thought. Rayanne and he probably had only a minute or two at most because in a town the size of Sweetwater Springs, the exact location of his hospital room likely wasn't much of a secret.

"How much backup's on the way?" Blue asked the deputy at the exact moment that Rayanne asked a version of the same. They were both still lawmen to the core, and whether Rayanne liked it or not, they were also on the same side.

For this, anyway.

"The sheriff and another deputy," Reed answered. "Both are Rayanne's brothers, and they're about five minutes out."

Good news about her brothers coming so fast. Blood kin meant they'd no doubt fight hard to make sure Rayanne stayed safe. Not so good news about the five minutes, though. That was more than enough time for the armed goons to get inside and do plenty of damage.

Blue glanced around and spotted exits at both ends of the corridor, which was lined with doors to patients' rooms on each side. He considered having Reed duck inside one of the rooms with Rayanne.

Any one of them but his own.

However, if the gunmen managed to pick the right door or if they just started randomly shooting, Rayanne could be hit or worse. Innocent bystanders could be, too. Right now he was a bullet magnet, but he wasn't sure he trusted this deputy who he didn't even know to be the one to protect Rayanne.

"Which exit is closest to the parking lot where those gunmen are?" Blue asked.

Reed pointed to the one to his left. Blue got all three of them moving in the opposite direction, and he hoped he could get Rayanne out of the hall before trouble arrived.

"You sure you're well enough to be doing this?" the deputy asked.

"No, he's not," Rayanne answered for him.

She was right. He wasn't well enough. Not well enough to fight off gunmen, anyway, but the pain zapping through him wouldn't stop him from getting Rayanne to safety.

Blue heard some sounds. Shrieks and shouts of people panicking. Someone had no doubt spotted the gunmen, and those sounds were far too close for comfort. He dropped back so that he'd be between the gunmen and Rayanne. He also kicked up the pace a notch, racing toward the exit.

"I'm sorry," he mumbled to Rayanne. He didn't have any experience with pregnant women, but he figured it wasn't a good thing to make her run like this. Of course, the stress wasn't good, either.

"Don't do anything that will make me regret this any more than I already do," she snapped.

That was Blue's intention. To do no more harm. Then once he had her safely tucked away, he could figure out who these morons were and what they wanted.

He could also deal with the baby then.

Just thinking about it now clouded his head. The pain did, too. And a clouded head was a good way to get them killed. He needed to think straight and be able to react.

They got to the exit just as Blue heard another unwelcome sound. Footsteps.

Not the ordinary variety, either.

These were the footsteps of someone flat-out running, and they seemed to be headed straight toward them.

Blue took out the *seemed* when he spotted one of them. There was no seeming about it. They were coming for them.

The first was big, bulky, mean looking.

And armed to the hilt with a gun in his hand and two others in holsters.

He looked a lot like the other two guys who came running in behind him.

Blue practically pushed Rayanne to the exit when the deputy opened the door. They raced with her.

Not a second too soon.

A shot cracked through the air.

Blue bit back the profanity when the bullet tore through a chunk of the doorjamb. Getting shot at twice in one day sure wasn't how he'd wanted this to play out.

"Hurry," Blue told Rayanne.

He shut the door. No lock. And the exit led them to a large covered area where vehicles dropped off patients. It was way too open for comfort, and Blue hoped there weren't any gunmen lurking outside waiting for them.

"My truck's this way," Reed said.

Blue hoped "this way" was close, because the armed idiots wouldn't be far behind. They ran, a lot faster than Blue's body wanted to run, and while they were mid-stride, the deputy took out his keypad and used it to open a silver truck.

"Stay ahead of me," Blue warned Rayanne. She didn't argue, thank goodness, and she held her hand protectively over her belly.

The moment they made it to the truck, Blue threw open the door and pushed Rayanne inside. Reed and he quickly followed, but Reed had barely managed to get the engine started when the gunmen bolted from the exit.

The three pivoted around, looking for them, and it didn't take them long to spot the truck. The goon in the lead took aim.

Fired.

Just as Reed peeled out of the parking lot.

The deputy thankfully didn't waste any time getting them the heck out of there. Blue spun in the seat, ready to return fire. Well, as ready as he could be considering he was dizzy as all get-out.

But he didn't have a shot, anyway.

It was too big a risk that he might hit someone other than the snake who'd just tried to kill him—again.

Reed practically flew out of the parking lot, and Blue heard and saw the cruiser then. Rayanne's brothers, no doubt. Maybe they'd be able to catch these dirt wads so that Blue could question them. Or beat them senseless for this stunt they'd just pulled.

"I don't think they're following us," Reed said, his attention volleying between the road and the parking lot. He reholstered his gun and took out his phone. Probably to call his boss, the sheriff, to let him know what was going on.

"Please tell me this jogged your memory," Rayanne mumbled through clenched teeth.

Blue had to shake his head. Man, that hurt, too.

However, his vision wasn't so blurry now that he couldn't see how pale Rayanne was. And that her hands were trembling. He'd worked with her on several cases and had never seen her like this.

But then, he'd never seen her pregnant, either.

It still wasn't a good time to think about it. Not with

those gunmen so close. However, Blue just couldn't shove it aside.

"You must hate me," Blue said, keeping watch around them in case those goons surfaced.

Her gaze whipped toward him, her eyes narrowed more than just a bit. "You're right about that. I do."

He wanted to think she was exaggerating, but he doubted she was. After all, he'd just endangered her life twice in a very short period of time. Then there was that part about sleeping with her and then running out on her without so much as a *thank you, ma'am*.

"I'll get to the bottom of this," Blue assured her, but judging from another of Rayanne's huffs, it was no reassurance at all. Of course, she didn't have a lot of reasons to trust him.

So Blue went in a different direction. One that he hoped would be common ground for them. "I need a truce, only until this mess in my head settles down, and I can figure out what's going on."

She certainly didn't agree.

He looked at her stomach again. "And I need you to be checked out by the doctor. All that running couldn't have been good for you and the baby."

"The running wasn't a problem. The doctor said I could keep up my workouts." Her mouth tightened as if she'd told him more than she meant to.

Still, it didn't matter. He'd call the doc first chance he got and have Rayanne checked out, because that hadn't been just a workout session.

"I'm not the one who needs to see the doctor," she mumbled, and she threw down the visor so Blue could get a glimpse at himself in the vanity mirror.

He was pale, beads of sweat dotted his face, and he

didn't look like an ATF agent ready to take down some killers. He looked like a man who'd just had surgery.

"I'm okay," he lied.

He probably wasn't even 50 percent yet, but he didn't have the luxury of recovering when there were gunmen out there who wanted to make his injuries even worse than they already were.

"I filled Cooper in," Reed said when he finished his call. "He's the sheriff and Rayanne's brother," he added to Blue. "Cooper wants us to wait at the sheriff's office while he and the others go after those men."

It was a good plan. Well, a safe one, anyway, for Rayanne. Blue hoped her brother would be able to catch them, but if the men hadn't followed Reed, then they'd probably already hightailed it out of town so they could regroup.

And come after him again.

Reed pulled his truck into the parking lot of the sheriff's office, and even though Blue didn't see anyone suspicious lurking around the building, he got Rayanne inside as quickly as possible. However, with the exception of a woman working at the front desk, the place seemed deserted, and that put him on edge again.

"We need to lock up," Blue told the deputy.

But Reed was already doing that. He obviously knew that they were vulnerable to another attack. Rayanne knew it, too, because she snatched her gun from him. At first he thought she'd done that just because she was upset that he'd taken it from her, but Blue realized he was wobbling.

Ah, heck.

"You need to sit down," Rayanne snapped, and she slid her arm around his waist, leading him into one of the offices. Sheriff Cooper McKinnon's nameplate was on the wall next to the door.

Disgusted with himself, Blue shook his head. "I should be the one protecting and taking care of you."

That earned him a predictable eye roll from her. "I'm pregnant, not incompetent."

Rayanne practically dumped him into a chair, then shut the door. Locked it, too, before she went to the window to make a cop's sweeping glance of the parking lot. No doubt checking to make sure those gunmen weren't lurking around out there.

Blue intended to do the same, but first he needed a gun. Since they were in the sheriff's office, he figured it wouldn't be hard to find one of those, and he started his search in the desk drawers.

Thankfully, the drawers were within reach, which meant he didn't have to stand up just yet. He really needed a moment or two to catch his breath and try to settle the tornado going on in his head.

Blue finally located a Smith & Wesson. Some extra ammo, too, which he crammed into his jeans pocket before he joined her at the window. He'd barely had time to get in place when there was a sharp knock at the door.

"We got another problem," Reed announced.

Rayanne hurried to the door, threw it open, and yeah, Blue could tell from the deputy's expression that something else had gone wrong.

Reed shook his head. "I don't know what you and Blue started, but all hell's breaking loose at the ranch. We need to get out there *now* because someone's trying to kidnap your sister."

Chapter Five

Rayanne had braced herself for more bad news, but she'd expected Reed to say that the gunmen had been spotted near her family's ranch. She darn sure hadn't expected to hear that someone had gone after Rosalie.

Someone who obviously had a death wish.

Rayanne wouldn't just stand by while someone hurt her twin sister.

"Let's go," Blue insisted.

Good thing, too. Her feet and mind had frozen in place, and it was the touch of Blue's hand on her arm that got her moving.

Rayanne's stomach was already churning. Her shoulders were still burning from tensing them so much, but she ran toward the back exit of the sheriff's office. Well, she started running, anyway, but like before, Blue played cowboy-bodyguard and positioned himself in front of her.

"I would suggest you stay here…" Blue mumbled. He didn't finish that.

Didn't have to.

Because there was no way she would stay put with Rosalie in danger. Of course, the trick would be to save her sister while not putting herself right back in the path of bullets. It was still a fairly new mind-set for her, but she had to think of the baby.

"What happened?" Rayanne asked Reed the moment they were inside the truck and on their way.

"A feed-delivery truck arrived, and your dad noticed something funny about the men."

"Roy," she automatically corrected. It'd been a while since she'd called him Dad, not since she'd been a kid, but Rayanne hated that she had even brought it up at a time like this. "Funny?" she questioned.

"Yeah. They weren't the usual guys who make the delivery. Your... Roy asked them to show some ID, and that's when they pulled guns on him. They demanded that he take them to Rosalie, and they said she'd be fine, as long as Blue and you cooperated, that is."

"Cooperated with what?" Blue and she asked in unison.

Reed shook his head. "They didn't get a chance to say. A ranch hand saw what was going on, and he got his gun. They exchanged a couple of shots, and the men started running toward the back pasture. The ranch hand and some others went after them."

Oh, mercy.

Rayanne's imagination was much too vivid, and she could see the whole thing playing out in her head. If any of her lawmen brothers had been there at the ranch, it would have made her breathe a little easier, but they were all in town looking for the men who'd come after Blue and her.

Maybe that'd all been a diversion.

So these jerks could kidnap Rosalie.

Her sister was a nurse and didn't even know Blue, but if there was even a shred of truth in what the men had told Roy, then they would have taken Rosalie hostage to manipulate Blue and her in some way.

"Was anyone hurt?" Rayanne asked, holding her breath.

"No. But Roy said it was a close call."

Like the one that Blue, Reed and she had just had at the hospital. Rayanne was getting sick and tired of the danger.

"You'd better get your memory back soon," she mumbled to Blue. "And hurry," Rayanne added to Reed, though the deputy was already doing just that.

It seemed to take an eternity, but the McKinnon ranch finally came into view. Rayanne didn't see any signs of chaos in the pastures. The horses were grazing as usual. But when Reed reached the house, she spotted the four ranch hands on the porch.

The men were all armed, standing guard.

Reed had barely brought the truck to a stop when she barreled out and raced toward the house. However, Rayanne had managed only a few steps when the front door opened, and her sister and Roy peered out. They both frantically motioned for her to get inside.

There was no sign of the gunmen, but it was obvious the danger hadn't passed. The goons wouldn't need Rosalie if they had Blue and her in their sights, and that was the reason Rayanne went back and helped Blue up the steps.

"Get inside," Blue snarled at her.

Again, he was doing that protector thing, and it set her teeth on edge. Of course, anything he did at this point would cause the same reaction.

"I'm sorry," Rayanne said when Rosalie's gaze met

hers. Her voice was all breath and clogged with way too much emotion.

"You have nothing to be sorry about," Rosalie scolded her, and pulled Blue and her into the foyer. "We're fine. Dad stopped them before they could get in the house."

Dad.

That was a different way of putting her teeth on edge. Rosalie had obviously gotten past the fact that twenty-three years ago, when Rayanne and she had been barely six, their parents had split over rumors that their mother had had an affair and then killed her lover.

Rayanne hadn't.

She was sure their mother was innocent of murdering her alleged lover, Whitt Braddock, but still Roy had sent her packing. Rosalie and her, too. Well, he hadn't done anything to stop their mother from taking them, anyway, despite having kept custody of his sons.

Rayanne didn't intend to let go of that old grudge anytime soon. Nor the grudge she was holding against Whitt's grown kids, his widow and even his elderly father for pressing for her mother's arrest.

Still, for now, she mumbled a thanks to Roy for protecting Rosalie.

"You must be Blue McCurdy," Rosalie said. "And you obviously need to sit down."

Rayanne still had her arm looped around him, but her sister took one look at Blue's face and lent him an arm, too. Together they led him toward the family room just off the foyer. Rosalie not only made sure he sat on the sofa, she began to examine the surgical wound beneath the bandage.

Only then did Rayanne see the blood seeping through

the bandage. It wasn't much but enough for her to suspect he'd popped a stitch or two.

"Blue McCurdy," Roy repeated.

Unlike Rosalie, he had no friendly, nurturing tone in his voice. Probably because he'd heard about Blue dumping her. Not from Rayanne, but Rosalie and he had no doubt had a few chats.

Roy and her mother, too.

He was apparently visiting her mother in jail, where she was awaiting trial. In the grand scheme of things, it was petty to think of it now, but seeing Roy always brought out the pettiness in her.

Roy kept staring at Blue. Nope, it was a glare. He likely felt the need to defend his daughter.

Well, she didn't want that from him, either.

What was it with these unwanted men in her life doing unwanted things? But that question vanished when Rosalie eased back Blue's bandage, and Rayanne got a glimpse of the angry-looking wound beneath.

"I'll get the first-aid kit," Rosalie said. "Some pain meds, too, and once the danger's passed, you'll need to go back to the hospital."

"No hospital and no pain meds," Blue insisted. "I need a clear head in case those men return."

"No sense arguing with him," Rayanne said to her sister. "He's hardheaded and won't listen even when he should."

"Like someone else I know," Rosalie mumbled, and headed out of the room.

The corner of Blue's mouth lifted. Enough of a smile for Rayanne's body to give her another punch of something else she didn't want. A reminder that his smile had always had her hormonal number.

Heck, who was she kidding?

Pretty much all of him could heat her up, but those days were long gone.

She hoped.

"I'll keep watch at the door," Roy said when Rayanne sank down on the sofa next to Blue, but he paused, glanced at her belly and looked on the verge of asking how she was. However, he must have realized it wasn't a good time to play daddy because he walked away.

"He's worried about you," Blue mumbled. "*I'm* worried about you?"

"I'm not the one who's been shot and is bleeding." And Rayanne had another look at the wound. Yep, he'd popped a stitch, all right.

"I'll be fine."

"Right. You can tell that lie to my sister, and she might believe it. I see otherwise."

That darn smile of his threatened to return. "Worried about me?"

Rayanne huffed a lot louder than necessary to show her disapproval. "Worried that I won't get you out of my life soon enough." She winced, paused. "I'm also worried that you won't get your memory back and be able to tell me why all of this is happening," she amended.

His gaze met hers, and the muscles in his jaw started to stir. "I haven't had time to give it a lot of thought, but there's only one reason I would have left you like that. And it would have been to protect you."

"Don't you think I know that?" she blurted out before she realized she was even going to say it.

Good grief.

It wasn't the time for *this* conversation, one that involved admitting that Blue had been a decent man. However, since she'd jumped off this particular cliff, Rayanne just kept going.

"Knowing that doesn't help. In fact, it only makes it worse. I'm a cop, Blue. I can take care of myself. You had a choice. Crush me or put me in danger. Trust me, I would have preferred the danger."

"Crush you?" he challenged.

Mercy, she hated that she had ever admitted something like that to him. Blue already had enough power over her with these blasted feelings that she still had for him.

Well, those feelings could take a hike, because she didn't want another dose of Blue.

Too bad her body had other ideas.

She still had the taste of him in her mouth. Literally. From the test kiss he'd laid on her at the hospital. To jog his memory, he'd said. It'd done a lot more than that.

It'd jogged hers.

And it had reminded Rayanne of why she'd landed in bed with him in the first place.

"What's going on in your head?" Blue asked in that deep Texas drawl that did pretty much the same thing to her body as his kiss had done.

Rayanne didn't even bother to scold her hormones, because it was clear that her body wasn't listening to a single warning she was doling out to it.

"If you were trying to protect me," she said, forcing her mind back on what it should be on, these blasted attacks, "then the questions are who's responsible and why?"

Blue didn't jump to answer, but he shook his head. "I don't know." He paused. "If I'd known you were pregnant—"

"Don't," she warned him.

"Don't shut me out of this," he warned her right back. "You've had weeks to come to terms with it, but I've only had an hour or so."

"Trust me, it'll take more than a few weeks to come to terms with it."

"You're not happy about the baby?" Blue came out and asked her.

"I didn't say that. I *am* happy." Scared out of her mind, too, but Rayanne kept that part to herself. She'd never admit that to him. To anyone. She already felt vulnerable enough without adding more to the mix.

"I'm sorry," he said, but didn't clarify exactly what he was apologizing for this time. Nor did Rayanne have time to ask, because her sister hurried back into the room.

Rosalie had not only the first-aid kit but a pan of water. "I called the doctor," she said, and got busy cleaning the wound. "After we're sure these would-be kidnappers are gone, he's coming out to check on you."

Good. Especially since Rayanne figured she stood no chance of talking Blue into returning to the hospital.

"Were you two talking about the baby?" Rosalie asked, volleying her attention between them and Blue's wound.

"No," Rayanne said at the same time that Blue answered, "Yes."

Rosalie made a sympathetic little hmm-ing sound, one that made Rayanne mentally curse herself. Rosalie's own newborn daughter had been stolen from the hospital only hours after she'd been born, and Rosalie would no doubt give up her life to get her baby back.

And here Rayanne was, not jumping for joy at the idea of motherhood.

Not on the outside, anyway, but Rayanne knew the bottom line here. She hadn't planned on this baby, hadn't planned on a baby, period, but she already loved this unborn hormone-generating machine with all her heart. And she would do anything to protect it.

Rayanne was so focused on that thought that she jumped a little when her phone buzzed. *Get a grip.*

"It's your boss," she told Blue when she saw Caleb's name on the screen. Blue took it from her and put the call on speaker.

"Caleb," Blue answered.

"Where the hell are you?" Caleb snapped.

"Someplace safe, I hope," he said. "Please tell me something else hasn't gone wrong."

"Wish I could say that, but I just had a conversation with a criminal informant. A reliable one." Caleb paused. Cursed. "Blue, you'd better get some rest. I've fought it and lost, and the department's given me no choice."

Blue did some cursing of his own. "What the heck are you talking about?"

Caleb cleared his throat. "I mean I'm going to have to arrest you."

Chapter Six

Blue glanced at the bottle of pills that Dr. Howland had left for him. When the doc had examined him about twelve hours earlier, he'd insisted that Blue take one every four hours to manage the pain. He hadn't and had somehow made it through the night in the guest room at the McKinnon ranch.

But Blue was certainly eyeing that bottle now.

The pain was a dull throb in his shoulder and head. Had been since he'd woken up in that hospital bed. And while Blue figured those little pills would take the edge off, they might also dull him enough so that he couldn't think his way out of this situation that was now his life.

Not a simple situation, either.

This one had plenty of layers.

One of those layers gave a sharp knock on the door and opened it before he could even issue the standard *come in*. Rayanne stepped inside, her gaze swinging from him to the pill bottle.

Then to his bare chest.

It was the second time in just as many days that she'd caught him shirtless. At least he had on jeans this time and not some butt-baring hospital gown. Hard to look like a man who could protect her while half-naked.

Blue considered reaching for his shirt, but Rayanne walked closer, a plastic bag looped over her wrist and a cup of coffee in each hand. "Thought it'd help with the headache," she said, and thrust one of the cups in his direction.

He darn sure didn't refuse it. His head might be a tangled heap of memories, but his body was screaming for caffeine. One sip, and he figured this just might be the cure for what ailed him.

Part of what ailed him, anyway.

Too bad he couldn't cure the rest of it with a few sips of strong coffee.

Rayanne dropped the plastic bag on the bed. "Your 'good-luck charms,'" she mumbled.

Blue glanced inside and saw that it was indeed his Stetson and his brown leather vest. Both had a few new scuffs, but he was glad to have them back. "Thanks."

"Thank the sheriff when you see him. He brought them when he finished his shift."

Which meant the CSIs likely hadn't found any trace or fibers that could help with the investigation. The possibility of that had been a long shot, anyway, but Blue had held out hope that there would be something to give them a lead.

"You never did say why the vest and hat were lucky," she commented. "Or maybe you don't remember?" Rayanne added with yet more skepticism. She clearly still didn't believe he had memory loss.

"I remember," he said under his breath. "It's a long story. I'll tell you about it sometime." Maybe.

Probably not, he amended, since he'd never told anyone. Some doors were best left closed.

Rayanne made a sound that could have meant anything, maybe even a twinge of hurt that he hadn't bared his soul. If she knew the story behind it, she'd thank him, since she didn't deal any better with emotional baggage than Blue did. Or at least she hadn't before the pregnancy.

"Rosalie will be up soon to check your bandage," she continued. "Since you refused to go back to the hospital, Dr. Howland wants her to call him if there's been any change in your condition. Is there a change?" she quickly tacked on to her update.

"Not with the memory. The pain's manageable." That last part was a downright lie, but if he said it enough, it might actually start to happen. Besides, Rayanne had enough to deal with without worrying that he was going to keel over.

Taking some long sips of coffee from her own cup, Rayanne sank down on the foot of his bed. Not too close to him, though. But it was close enough for him to notice that she wasn't drinking coffee but rather chocolate milk.

She looked tired and amazing all at the same time. She was wearing her usual jeans and a plain tan shirt that hugged her body just enough for him to see another layer to this complex situation.

The baby bump.

"We're not going to discuss that now," she said, obviously following his gaze. "Or that," she added when his wandering eyes landed on her mouth.

Blue couldn't help it. He smiled. Even with the danger breathing down their proverbial necks, Rayanne could do that to him.

Sadly, his smile seemed to only rile her even more.

"Caleb already called earlier this morning," she informed him.

Ah, so that was the source of this particular riling.

Well, it must have been darn early, because it was barely eight o'clock now.

"And?" Blue asked when she didn't continue.

"He'll be here in about an hour, and yes, he still says he'll arrest you, that he doesn't have a choice. The powers that be believe you're a dirty agent."

Not exactly a surprise. Before he'd finally had to collapse in bed, Blue had spent a few hours trying to sort out why a criminal informant had claimed Blue was on the payroll of criminal kingpin Rex Gandy. He wasn't any closer to learning the truth than he had been last night, but he'd need to learn it soon if he hoped to stop Caleb from hauling him into custody.

"If Caleb's superiors are taking the word of this CI," Rayanne continued, "then they must have some kind of proof to go along with it."

Blue felt as if she'd slugged him. "We're back to you thinking I'm a criminal?"

She lifted her shoulder. "I think the CI might think that. Probably because you gave him a reason to believe it. Like maybe some kind of deep-cover investigation that you didn't bother to tell anyone about. Something that would make you look like a criminal."

Blue couldn't dismiss that, but without details and proof, he didn't have a way to clear his name. "Whatever it is, it obviously involves you."

Rayanne stared into her cup of milk. Nodded. "Let's play this through and see if it jogs anything in your memory. Five months ago something happened, something big enough and dangerous enough for you to start this investigation that's brought you here. We'd just finished that case in Appaloosa Pass, so maybe it's connected to that?"

It was his turn to nod. "If so, then it's linked to Gandy because we arrested one of his so-called lieutenants."

It'd been a solid arrest, too. His team and Rayanne had found not just a stash of illegal weapons but plenty of paperwork and even a witness who could put the lieutenant away for life.

Except the guy's life hadn't lasted that long.

He'd gotten into a fight during lockup and had been killed by another prisoner. Yet something else Blue needed to investigate. Had the lieutenant been killed in a jail fight or had he been targeted for a kill because of things he could have told the Justice Department?

Things about his boss, Rex Gandy.

Blue paused, thought about that some more. "So maybe this is a simple case of revenge. Gandy wanted to get back at us for the arrest or even the death of his thug cohort, and he set me up to make it look like I'm a criminal."

Rayanne made a sound to indicate she agreed with that. "One who'd accept a contract to kill me."

Yeah, and that was where their theory fell plenty short. "Gandy must have known that I wouldn't kill the woman carrying my baby."

"He probably didn't know I was pregnant." She gave him a quick glance. "I haven't told anyone other than family, and I've been trying to keep it hidden."

Blue had several questions about that but decided to go for the obvious one. "Why?"

Another shrug. "I just wasn't ready to deal with the questions yet."

Yeah, because questions about the baby meant questions about him, too. Not that he needed it, but it was yet more proof of how much he'd hurt her.

And how much she detested him for hurting her.

Heck, he detested himself, too, and the only thing that would make this better was for him to learn why he'd walked out on her in the first place. Even if he'd had doubts about sleeping with her, he wasn't the sort to go slinking out on a walk of shame. And he especially wouldn't have done that to Rayanne.

Rayanne's gaze came to Blue's, and this time it wasn't for just a glimpse. Their eyes met, held. "Swear to me that this memory thing isn't an act."

The woman certainly knew how to keep him on his toes. "Why in the name of heaven would I fake that?"

"So that you can keep the details of whatever you're involved in to yourself," she readily answered, which meant she'd thought this through.

He huffed, cursed. "There's no reason for me to do that." Blue pointed to the bandage on his shoulder. "This bullet could have hit you. Trust me, I want to remember anything and everything about the idiots who put you in danger."

And he intended to stop it.

That stopping started with his figuring out how to get Caleb off his back. Then he needed to find their attackers and force them to talk. The first was doable.

Maybe.

The second would likely take some solid detective work and a hefty dose of divine intervention.

Blue forced himself to get up. He was moving a little easier now, and the caffeine had indeed helped with his throbbing head, but he required more than moving just a little easier. He needed a break in this case, and he needed it yesterday.

"I'll make some more calls," he explained. Maybe to

some other CIs who could perhaps explain what the heck he'd been doing for the past five months. Someone out there had to know. He doubted he'd been living in a hole in the ground all this time.

Rayanne took her phone from her pocket and handed it to him. He reached for it, wobbled just a little, and lightning fast, Rayanne set her cup on the floor and came off the bed to take hold of him.

Just like that, he was in her arms. Well, almost. She slid her arm around his waist, putting them side to side with a whole lot of touching. His body didn't seem to understand that this was just part of her nursing duties.

"Best not to get any more head injuries," she mumbled. "And if you smile, I might hurt you."

Oh, he smiled, all right, because he was obviously losing it. The proof of that was the stupid stirring in his body, especially one part of him that thought he might get lucky. He wasn't in any shape to get lucky, even if Rayanne had been willing.

And she clearly wasn't.

"Just resist the temptation," she snarled.

He wasn't sure if they were talking about his smile or something else. "Trust me, I've had a lot of practice resisting you."

She blinked, stared up at him. "Excuse me?"

Blue was surprised that she was surprised.

"You think all that time we worked on those cases together that my mind was solely on the job? It wasn't," he assured her before she could respond, though it looked as if she was too thunderstruck to say much of anything. "I've been attracted to you since day one."

For just a heartbeat, she looked a little pleased about

that, but then Rayanne shook her head. "How can you remember that?"

"Oh, I remember some things."

Things that caused him to stray into the stupid realm again, because he brushed a kiss on her cheek. Thank goodness it was only her cheek, because he could have sworn he saw little lightning bolts zing through her eyes.

She let go of him so fast that he had no choice but to sit back on the bed or he would have fallen. "Blue, this can't happen again."

He nodded. "I know."

And he did.

Didn't he?

Well, his brain knew that it was a dumb thing to do, but his brain and other parts of him hadn't exactly made some good decisions lately.

Cursing that and himself, he put Rayanne's phone on the nightstand, took the clean shirt that Rosalie had left for him and put it on, trying not to wince or make some other sound to prove he'd lied about the pain. However, before he could even button up and start those calls, her phone rang, and he saw Caleb's name on the screen.

Blue hit the speaker button so he could talk while he finished dressing. "Still plan on arresting me?"

"The criminal informant won't back down. He's pressing for the charges against you, and he added more than his sworn testimony to the table." Caleb paused. "He's got proof."

That brought Rayanne to her feet, and she moved closer to the phone. "You'd trust so-called proof from a criminal informant over the word of one of your agents?"

"I would if the agent can't vouch for what he's been doing for the past five months." Caleb paused again. "The

CI has photos of Blue meeting with a guy named Burrell Parker. He's a low-life arms dealer, and we're almost positive that he's the one who arranged for the hit on you."

Blue didn't have to think long and hard about that. "Maybe I was meeting with this guy Parker because I got wind of the hit and was trying to stop it."

"Maybe, but you took money from him. The CI got a picture of that, too. And before you say anything, yeah, it smacks of a setup, but I can't just dismiss it. I need to bring you in and try to clear all of this up."

Blue had a different notion about that. "I'd rather not be behind bars while you're clearing up things that affect me and the people around me. I need to help."

"Then help by telling me why you met with Parker," Caleb fired back.

"I don't know." And he cursed himself again. This blasted concussion was beyond an inconvenience. "But I'm guessing Parker works for Rex Gandy like those thugs who tried to kill Rayanne and me yesterday?"

"No," Caleb argued. "Well, if he does, there's no obvious proof or connection with Gandy, but Parker had a connection with someone else we know. Your former partner and friend, Woody Janson."

Of all the things Blue had expected Caleb to say, that wasn't one of them.

"Woody's missing," he reminded his boss. Or at least, that was what Rayanne had told him.

"Yeah, missing under suspicious circumstances. You remember he phoned you right before you, too, disappeared under that same cloud of suspicion. What I need to know is what you two discussed that night."

Blue tried again to pick through that whirl of thoughts in his aching head and came up blank. "I don't know."

"I don't, either," Rayanne volunteered, "but I'm pretty sure that Woody called because he was in some kind of trouble. What about the CI? Did he say where Woody was?"

"Like the two of you, he claims he doesn't know, but Woody's in a couple of those pictures of Blue meeting with Parker when the hit on Rayanne was arranged."

Again, Blue hadn't seen that coming, and he wished he could force the memories to come. But the more he pushed, the worse the pain got.

"We need to find Woody," Rayanne mumbled.

"*I* need to find him," Blue corrected. To get some answers about that meeting that had put him in hot water. "It's too risky for you to be involved in this."

A burst of air left her mouth, and it was most definitely not a laugh. "I'm already involved. There's a hit order out on me, and just because you didn't fill it, that doesn't mean it'll go away."

"She's right," Caleb said. "But the question is, why was the hit ordered on her in the first place?"

Blue had already gotten a headache over that question, too, and it'd been the very thing on his mind when he'd fallen asleep the night before. "Someone must have thought I told her something she shouldn't know. Maybe something about this thug Parker. And that means I want to talk to him."

"I'm already working on getting him in for questioning, but you won't have any part of that. Rayanne, either. Look, I'm trying to buy you some time, Blue, but I've got people breathing down my neck. They want you brought in now."

Blue hated to play the pain card here, but it wasn't a total act. "What if I'm still under care of a doctor? I had a bullet dug out of my shoulder just yesterday, and I'm thinking the last thing the doctor would want is for me to be hauled off to jail."

Where he wouldn't be able to work on clearing his name. Or where he wouldn't be able to protect Rayanne. Something she wasn't going to like, but Blue didn't plan to give her a say in the matter.

Caleb didn't jump to agree, so Blue continued bargaining with him. "Give me forty-eight hours."

Now Caleb reacted. He cursed again. "Please tell me you don't want that time so you can interfere with an active investigation where you clearly have a conflict of interest?"

Now it was Blue who didn't jump to answer. "You want the truth?"

"No," Caleb said. Then he groaned. "Don't do anything that'll make me regret this, and I'll see what I can do about getting you those twenty-four hours."

"I asked for forty-eight."

But Blue was talking to himself because Caleb had already hung up.

Blue stared at the phone a moment and considered calling his boss back to push for more time. However, he had more important things to do. Like arrange for some extra protection for Rayanne and her sister since these bozos had already tried to use Rosalie to get to them.

"How much are you going to fight me on this?" Blue came out and asked Rayanne.

She stared at him, put her hands on her hips. "Probably a lot. Why? What do you *think* you're planning to do?"

Oh, yes. She'd fight him, all right. "I want Rosalie and you to move to a safe house."

"And you?" Rayanne tipped her head to his bandage.

"Of the three of us, you're the one who's least capable of fighting off bad guys."

"You're wrong. I've got plenty of incentive to fight off anyone who comes after you." Now he did some head tipping. To her stomach.

She groaned. "I knew this would happen, but I want it to stop. You left, and I learned how to get along without you. It stays that way, got that?"

Blue would have assured her that she was wrong and that he didn't intend to agree to her *got that?* but there was some movement in the open doorway. He looked up, expecting to see Rosalie with the supplies to change his bandage, but it was her brother Colt.

"You two need to table this discussion," Colt said, not exactly in a friendly tone, either, "because someone just drove up. He says his name is Rex Gandy."

"Gandy's here?" Rayanne blurted out, already hurrying to the window.

Blue hurried, too. Well, as much as he could, and even though it earned him a huff, he stepped in front of Rayanne. He had no trouble spotting the man leaning against the white Cadillac that was parked in the drive at the front of the house. Bulky build, salt-white hair and a chunky cigar clamped between his teeth.

Yeah, it was Gandy, all right.

If the man was nervous about walking into the lion's den, he sure didn't show it. He appeared to be lounging, his legs stretched out in front of him, not paying any attention to the two ranch hands.

Both had guns trained on the man.

As if he knew he was being watched, Gandy looked up, his gaze sliding across the windows. The sliding stopped when his attention landed on Blue.

He smiled.

It was even more motivation for Blue to get Rayanne moved to a safe house. He didn't want men like Gandy being able to get this close to her. Heck, a hundred miles was too close for this snake.

"What does he want?" Blue asked Colt.

"Says he wants to talk to you."

Blue kept his stare fixed on the man. "Did he give any reason why I'd *want* to talk to him?"

"Yeah. Gandy says he's here to help you. In fact, he claims he's got exactly what you need to clear your name."

That got Blue's attention, but he was betting that Gandy hadn't shared what he had with Colt.

If Gandy had anything at all, that is.

This could be some kind of ploy to draw them out into the open.

"You want to talk to him or not?" Colt asked.

Blue nodded and grabbed his vest and Stetson. "But not here. Let's haul him down to the sheriff's office and see what this piece of slime has to say."

Chapter Seven

Twenty-four hours.

With everything so crazy around them, that was what Rayanne's mind kept going back to—the very short deadline that Caleb had doled out to Blue. The minutes were just ticking away, and if Caleb followed through on his threat to arrest Blue, then he would soon be hauled off to jail.

Blue had done plenty of things to rile her.

And crush her.

However, she hadn't seen a shred of proof, not proof that she'd believe, anyway, that he'd intended to carry out the hit on her.

Now they were on this too-tight time limit, and despite how she felt about the scumbag waiting in the interview room of the sheriff's office, if Rex Gandy could clear any of this up, then she would welcome anything he could give them.

Not because Blue was the father of her child.

No.

It was because the sooner they got all of this cleared up, the sooner Blue could leave. Again. And the sooner her life could get back to the seminormal it'd been before he'd reappeared in her life.

Rayanne moved out of the doorway of the deputy's office where Blue was finishing up some phone calls, and she went across the hall to the observation room. Blue hadn't wanted her to be involved when he talked to Gandy. Rayanne hadn't exactly wanted that, either, but she also didn't want to be sheltered like a damsel in distress.

Even if that label did sort of fit her these days.

She wanted to have an active part in identifying the men who'd taken shots at Blue and her, and that part started right here with Gandy.

"You're scowling," she heard someone say, and she looked up to see Seth standing in the doorway of the observation room.

Seth was the lone black suit in a sea of jeans, cowboy boots and rodeo buckles. Mr. FBI with the star-quarterback looks. And even though she didn't like that he'd no doubt put aside plenty of work to be here, she was thankful he'd done that for her. She was even more thankful there was no need to tell him that.

Saying thanks wasn't her strong suit.

Hearing it wasn't Seth's.

Her brother walked closer, until he was shoulder to shoulder with her, and he looked through the two-way mirror at Gandy, who was seated at the table.

Not alone.

Gandy had two lawyers flanking him, both dressed in cowboy duds like their boss. Both looking as much like snake-oil salesmen as he did.

"When's the last time you combed your hair?" Seth asked, glancing at her.

Rayanne frowned. "When's the last time you had a busted lip, because you're working on one."

It was a customary sister-brother exchange, no doubt something Seth had started to get her mind off her troubles—both Blue and the ones on the other side of the glass. However, Rayanne ran her hand over her hair and shoved some of the strands back into her ponytail.

Fixing herself up a little had nothing to do with Blue, she assured herself, and she was almost certain she believed it.

"How are you?" Seth asked.

He didn't look at her stomach, but Rayanne knew what he meant. "I'm taking my prenatal vitamins," she settled for saying. "Drinking my milk and eating right."

"Dodging bullets, too, from what I hear." He paused. "I agree with Blue. You need to go to a safe house."

Great. Now they were ganging up on her. "When did you talk to Blue?"

"Last night after the doctor left the ranch." It was Seth's turn to scowl. "I told Blue if he hurts you again, that I'd kill him."

Oh, man. "You what? You had no right—"

"It's a brother's right." He leaned in, dropped a kiss on her cheek. "But I gotta tell you, I don't think he's got any plans to hurt you. And I don't believe for one minute that he was at the ranch to carry through on a hit. I think he was there to save you."

Because she was riled at Seth's threat, she wanted to snarl and argue, but she couldn't. Not about that, anyway.

"I don't need you to fight my battles," she grumbled.

"No, but I do enjoy seeing you riled, so I'll try it more often." With that brotherly jab, Seth strolled away, and it was only after he was out of the doorway that she saw Blue standing there.

"Everything okay?" Blue asked, eyeing Seth with

slightly narrowed, cautious eyes. The way a man would eye a coiled diamondback rattler.

"Far from it. Apparently, Seth wants to play the part of my personal protector, too." She paused, reined in her temper. "He threatened to kill you, but you know he wouldn't do that, right?"

Blue lifted his shoulder, winced a little. Something he'd been doing not only on the ride over but since they'd arrived. She made a mental note to call the doctor and have him check those stitches again.

"Seth's your brother," Blue said. "He doesn't want you hurt."

That didn't excuse Seth's Neanderthal approach to interfering in his kid sister's life, and she hoped her huff conveyed not only that but the end of this particular conversation.

"Are you ready to go in there and find out what Gandy claims he has?" she asked. She stared at the bruise on his head. It was a nasty purple color today and went from his hairline to the edge of his eyebrow. "Or have you come to your senses and are willing to let the sheriff or one of the deputies do their jobs and deal with this jerk?"

"No. I haven't come to my senses." And Blue added one of those half smiles that Rayanne wished she could wipe off his face.

Or at least share with him.

She was too worried to smile about anything, and she hated that scum like Gandy could hold Blue's badge in the palm of his sweaty hand.

"I just talked to Burrell Parker," Blue said, glancing down at the notepad he was holding.

Rayanne pulled in her breath. She had known he was

on the phone, but she hadn't guessed he was talking to the very man who might have ordered a hit on her. "And?"

"And he denied everything."

She shook her head. "But there are photos of you meeting with him."

"Parker says those are pictures of me threatening to blow his head off because I wouldn't give him information about my missing partner, Woody Janson."

Rayanne took a moment to process that. It made sense. From everything she'd read about him, Parker was dealing in illegal arms, and it was the sort of thing Blue and his former partner would have investigated.

"You don't remember talking to Parker about Woody?" she asked.

"No, but the ATF had already accessed Woody's phone records. The calls end the same time he disappeared, but prior to that, Woody apparently had several conversations with Parker. I don't know about what."

"But before the concussion, you would have known about the conversations," she finished for him. "And you would have most certainly asked Parker about them."

He nodded. "I did ask him, and Parker says he has no idea what happened to Woody but that Gandy might know."

Rayanne huffed. Of course he would say that. Parker and Gandy were rivals in the gun business, and he'd say or do anything not only to take suspicion off himself but also to set up Gandy.

However, that didn't mean Parker was lying.

"Caleb's bringing Parker in for questioning," Blue continued. "He might be able to get something from Parker that we can use."

Something to help clear Blue's name and end the danger. Rayanne welcomed that with open arms.

Blowing out a long breath, she raked her hand through her hair, only to remember that she'd just fixed it. Sort of. She made another attempt to fix it.

"Ironic that when I woke up yesterday morning, I thought the worst thing I'd have to deal with was my mother's upcoming murder trial," she mumbled.

And while that was horrible, it still paled in comparison to the danger all of this could pose to the baby. Her mother still stood a strong chance of being found not guilty. At least to Rayanne's way of thinking, anyway. But the threat to the baby was immediate, and there didn't seem to be a reprieve in sight.

"I promise, I'll fix this," Blue said. It was a promise he likely couldn't keep, but for some stupid reason, Rayanne latched on to it.

However, she didn't latch on to him.

When he moved closer as if he might give her a hug or something, she stepped back. Best to keep not just physical distance between them but some emotional space, as well. Her hormones were still playing tricks on her, and her body might think a hug from Blue was a whole lot more.

And it couldn't be.

Blue mumbled something about wishing him luck, and he walked out. A moment later Rayanne watched as he walked into the interview room with Gandy.

When his attention landed on Blue, Gandy chuckled, his gut wobbling. He hooked his thumbs behind the grapefruit-sized rodeo buckle and leaned back in the chair.

"Somebody messed you up bad, didn't they, boy?"

Gandy said. "Bruised up your pretty face, and if I'm not mistaken, that's a bandage beneath your shirt. Hurt much?"

"Yeah," Blue readily admitted, doling out a dose of the same cocky tone that Gandy was using. "And I'm thinking that the somebody who did this to me might be you."

If Gandy was alarmed by that accusation, he didn't show it. He dismissed it with the flick of his hand. "I got better things to do than take shots at a rogue gun agent and his deputy girlfriend."

Well, at least Gandy hadn't said *pregnant* girlfriend, but that didn't mean he didn't know. And if he knew, he could somehow use her and the baby to get to Blue.

If this was all some kind of cat-and-mouse game to do just that.

"You said you had proof to clear my name," Blue reminded him, dropping down in the chair on the opposite side of the table from Gandy and his legal entourage.

"What, no small talk?" Gandy joked.

"We could stretch this out. I could also find a reason to arrest you. Any reason."

That got Gandy's lawyers whispering to him, but the man waved them off and leaned forward, propping his elbows on the table. "I don't want to get involved in this." For the first time since this conversation had started, Gandy seemed serious.

"You're the one who came to the McKinnon ranch looking for me," Blue reminded him. "You've involved yourself in this already."

"Yeah, but only so I could make sure I don't get blamed for the bullet that somebody put in you yesterday."

Blue met the man's stare with one of his own. "It was your hired thugs who attacked me."

Gandy quickly shook his head. "They haven't worked for me in a while. Not for Parker, either. Let's just say that trio of idiots was freelancing."

"Who hired them?" Blue pressed. "And you'd better not say it was me."

"No, it wasn't you." He reached for his jacket pocket but stopped when Blue pulled his gun. "You're a mite touchy, aren't you? I've already been frisked, and I'm not packing heat. This bulge around my waist is just from too many rare T-bones and plenty of beer."

The joking tone was back, but Gandy still waited until Blue had given him a go-ahead nod before he took out the small padded envelope and tossed it on the table between them.

"What's that?" Blue studied it, but he didn't touch it.

"It's surveillance images of your meeting with Parker. The very one that your boss has pictures of."

Blue lifted the edge of the envelope and Rayanne caught a glimpse of the flash drive inside.

"How'd you get this?" Blue asked, taking the question right out of her mouth.

Gandy flexed his eyebrows. "I like to keep my eyes on my competition. Now, you likely can't use that as evidence, because it wasn't exactly obtained with Parker's permission, but if you listen to it, you'll hear that it clears your name."

"Listen to it?" Blue repeated.

Gandy grinned. "It has audio, and it's real clear, too. Your boss can hear you threaten Parker if he doesn't man up about your missing agent friend. Of course, that's just a summary of the threat. You used a lot more words and some very creative profanity."

So Parker had been telling the truth. Gandy, too.

About this, anyway.

If that surveillance flash drive was what Gandy said it was, then it would indeed stop Blue from being arrested.

Gandy's attention stayed fixed on the nasty bruise on Blue's head. "You do remember this conversation with Parker, right?"

"Sure," Blue lied, and that came easily, too.

Of course, he'd had a lot of practice with deception during his deep-cover assignments. However, it did make him wonder if in that whirl of memories, his deep-cover lies were getting mixed up with the truth. Not good. They needed him to be able to sort through this and help identify the person who'd hired those thugs.

"So why help me?" Blue asked Gandy. It was yet something else that Rayanne wanted to know, too.

Gandy didn't jump to answer, and he eased back into his chair. "Because this is gonna turn into a big stinkin' mess, and I don't want to be part of it." The man's gaze went to the mirror. "I'm guessing your girl's there, watching."

"My *girl* is none of your business," Blue snapped.

"Yeah, she is. Well, she is in that whatever I'm about to take out of the other pocket pertains more to her than to you."

That brought Blue to his feet. "What the heck are you talking about now?"

Gandy took that something out of his pocket. A photo. And as with the flash drive, he slid it Blue's way. "You won't recognize the fellow in the photo, but your girl will."

Rayanne knew Blue wasn't going to like this, but she hurried straight toward the interview room and threw open the door. She got the exact reaction that she expected.

Blue scowled at her, mumbled something and stepped in front of her.

Gandy just grinned that stupid grin and slid the photo in her direction. Despite Blue being in her way, Rayanne got a good look at it by peering over his shoulder.

It was a grainy shot probably taken from a long-range lens. Two men seated at a booth in what appeared to be a café. Her attention first went to the man on the left.

And her stomach tensed.

It was one of the men who'd tried to kill them. He was dead now, lying in the city morgue, but it still sent an ice-cold chill through her to see that face.

That chill got worse when she saw the other man in the photo.

"No," she heard herself mumble, and despite Blue's maneuvering to stop her, she got around him and picked up the picture for a closer look.

"You know that man?" Blue asked her.

Rayanne nodded, didn't trust her voice to say more right away.

"That's Wendell Braddock," Gandy explained for her. "He's the father of the man who Rayanne's mother is accused of murdering."

Blue cursed and stepped in front of her again. "Please tell me you got that picture from the surveillance flash drive and that it has audio to go along with it," he said to Gandy.

Gandy shook his head. "Afraid not on that one. But from what I heard, your girl here is smart. A deputy sheriff and all. Shouldn't take much for her to come up with a reason why Wendell Braddock would be talking to a hired gun and why the Braddock patriarch wants her dead and buried."

No. It didn't take Rayanne long at all.

Wendell was an old man, in his mid-eighties, but he was rich, the owner of not just a successful ranch but several equally successful companies.

And he hated her and her family.

Rayanne was well aware of that hatred, not just from Wendell but from the entire Braddock clan. Still, it was a shock to see the man in that photo maybe cutting a deal with someone he was hiring to murder her.

"Must be hard," Gandy went on, speaking to Rayanne. "Your mother in jail, and Wendell's grandson holding the keys to her cell."

Blue shot her a questioning glance, and she nodded. "My mother's at the county jail in the town of Clay Ridge, and Aiden Braddock is the county sheriff."

Gandy smiled. "Aiden's daddy is Whitt, the man Jewell's accused of murdering, and his granddaddy is Wendell. A bit of a tangled mess, huh?"

Blue shook his head. "Why the heck was that allowed to happen?"

"Because Mom couldn't be held here in Sweetwater Springs, where her son Cooper is the sheriff," Rayanne explained. "The alternative was to have her sent to another county, and she didn't want that, because she didn't want to be that far from the ranch."

It was something that still didn't sit right with Rayanne. That being close was nice for visits, but it had come at a high price, with her mother being in the custody of a man who no doubt hated her. It was on a long list of things that troubled her about her mother's situation.

Including this latest development—that photo of Wendell.

"This explains why those men tried to kidnap Rosalie," she mumbled to Blue. "So Wendell could get revenge against my mother."

"It *could* mean that, or not," Blue argued. "Remember, a photo made it look as if I was meeting with someone to set up a hit. Without audio to go along with that, we have no idea what that meeting was about. Heck, it could have been just to set up Wendell so it takes our attention off the real person behind this."

Blue shot a cold, accusing look at Gandy.

It was a reasonable argument, especially since Gandy had been the one to give them the photo, but now it was Rayanne who shook her head. "I have to talk to Wendell."

Of course, Blue stopped her from bolting out of the room. Probably because she looked a little crazy and ready to do something totally stupid—like confront Wendell at gunpoint and demand the truth.

Blue first grabbed the surveillance flash drive that Gandy had given them, then took her by the arm and led her out into the hall. Another good idea, since this wasn't a conversation that she wanted to have in front of Gandy. He was practically gloating and clearly enjoyed being the bearer of bad news.

About this, anyway.

Maybe Gandy had been the one to set all of this up after all. If so, it was working. Wendell was now at the top of her suspect list. However, that didn't mean she would erase Gandy from that list anytime soon.

"This could be exactly what Wendell wants you to do," Blue said the moment that he had the interview room door shut. "If you go after him half-cocked, he can have you arrested. Heck, he could have all of us arrested, since you know we'd stand up for you."

Yes, she did know that.

And Rayanne cursed that and everything else she could think of to curse. "Wendell wants to punish my mother by hurting Rosalie and me."

Blue took her by the shoulders and forced her to look him in the eyes. "If that's really his plan, then don't give him the chance to do that. We'll find the third surviving gunman, and we'll get him to talk. If Wendell hired him, then we'll prove it."

She hated that he could be so darn logical at a time when she just wanted to grab Wendell or Gandy by their collars and force them to talk. Considering that Blue was sporting an injury that one of them had perhaps given him, he no doubt wanted the same thing.

"Everything okay?" Cooper asked.

Rayanne had been so caught up in her anger and the conversation with Blue that she hadn't even heard him come up behind them.

"You need to bring Wendell Braddock in for questioning," she said, handing the photo to Cooper.

As she'd done, he studied it a moment before the muscles tightened in his jaw. "Yeah, I'll bring him in." Cooper looked up from the photo, his attention going back to Blue. "You finished with Gandy?"

Blue nodded. "He had this flash drive that proves I'm innocent. I need to get a copy of it to my boss ASAP so he can kill the arrest warrant."

"I can do that for you, if you like," Cooper offered. "I can also finish up the interview and ask the Rangers to help us keep an eye on Gandy, if you want to go ahead and take Rayanne to the hospital."

"The hospital?" she snapped.

Cooper checked over his shoulder as if making sure that no one was within earshot. No one was. "Doc How-

land called and said you never showed up for an ultrasound that he said he told you that he wanted to do after
the shooting incident."

Rayanne released the breath she'd sucked in. For a moment, one horrifying moment, she'd thought Cooper was
going to say there was something wrong with the baby.

"I figured I could have the ultrasound after things
settled down," Rayanne said. "Besides, I'm feeling fine."

Cooper gave her a flat look. "You might deliver that
baby before things 'settle down.'"

Not exactly a comforting thought, because it was the
truth.

"Go to the hospital," Cooper insisted, and he turned
his attention back to Blue. "You're not looking too steady
on your feet, either. Wouldn't hurt for you to at least have
another checkup."

He was right—Blue didn't look too steady. It was a
generous offer for Cooper to tie up loose ends for them,
especially considering he had to have a ton to do in order
to wrap up the paperwork on the attacks.

And given the fact that he was barely on speaking
terms with her.

However, she'd always heard that her estranged brother
was a decent sheriff, so maybe this was all about doing
his job and had nothing to do with family or favors.

"Thanks," Blue said, handing him the flash drive.

Cooper's attention slid back to her again. "You won't
go after Wendell," he said, and it wasn't a suggestion. He
was sounding more and more like the sheriff that he was.

Or a very stubborn brother.

She already had one of those. Didn't need another one.

"She won't go after him," Blue answered.

Rayanne huffed. "I'm standing right here. I can speak for myself."

Both of them stared at her so long that the stares turned to glares. "All right," she mumbled. "I won't go after Wendell." Not today, anyway. "But if he's behind this—"

"Then I'll arrest him," Cooper assured her. "Just because we're not on the same side when it comes to Jewell, that doesn't mean I won't do my job."

She nodded, eventually, and mumbled a thanks.

"One of the deputies is at the hospital, tying up some loose ends," Cooper added. "If you run into any trouble there, he'll be able to respond."

Rayanne felt obligated to issue another thanks. A first. She wasn't accustomed to doling out multiple thanks to someone who disliked her mother as much as she loved her, but this was far from normal.

Blue got her moving toward the back exit, and once again he played the part of the supercop by getting in front of her and taking the first look out into the parking lot. He took his time checking things out, too, and after some long moments, he hurriedly ushered them into her truck. He got behind the wheel, of course, even though she was in better driving shape than he was.

"You should have told me that the doctor wanted to do an ultrasound," Blue mumbled.

Rayanne braced herself for a lecture, and she was ready to lecture him right back. After all, Blue had refused to go back to the hospital despite the fact he was only twenty-four hours out of surgery.

"Would you mind if I go to the ultrasound with you?" he added, driving out of the parking lot.

Oh, so no lecture. But it was something that still

caused a rise in her emotions. Viewing an ultrasound together seemed like something a couple would do.

And they weren't a couple.

But there was another angle to this. Rayanne really didn't want to see the doctor alone. She'd never thought of herself as a scaredy-cat, and she honestly believed all was well with the baby.

Or maybe that was just what she needed to believe.

Still, she could get news that would be impossible to take. News that was too painful even to consider, that there might indeed be something wrong.

"You can be there for the ultrasound," she finally said. "But this doesn't mean anything."

Blue made that little sound of amusement. "Sure it does. It means everything. Thanks."

Maybe he didn't realize how much that rankled her. Okay, he probably did. Blue could usually manage to get a rise out of her.

And surprise her.

"I figured you'd be running for the hills by now," she mumbled. "I'm sure having a baby wasn't on your to-do list."

He glanced at her stomach but didn't get a chance to confirm or deny what she'd just tossed at him, because her phone rang.

"Cooper," she said after looking at the screen. Something had better not have gone wrong with Gandy. Rayanne pressed the button to put the call on speaker.

"Get out of your truck now!" Cooper shouted. "I just got a call that there's a bomb in it."

Chapter Eight

Blue slammed on the brakes, drew his gun and reached for Rayanne to pull her from the truck.

But then he stopped.

Not easy to come to a standstill, because he was fighting his instincts to run like the devil and get Rayanne to safety. It was the same for Rayanne. She already had a death grip on her gun and had latched on to the door handle.

"This could be a trick to get us out in the open," Blue reminded Cooper, though he figured the sheriff had already thought of that. "How credible is the call?"

"No way of knowing." Cooper cursed. "The name and number were blocked. Do what your gut tells you, and I'll get someone over there to help you ASAP."

"We're on Main Street," Rayanne told him. "Between the hardware and the antiques stores."

She looked at Blue, her eyes wide and her breath already gusting. Obviously, Rayanne was waiting for him to go with his gut.

"We're getting out now," Blue insisted. "Keep watch around us."

He would definitely do the same, and even though he

was going with that whole gut-trust thing, Blue hoped this wasn't a huge mistake.

After he made sure no one was lying in wait to attack them, he threw open the truck door and pulled Rayanne out on the driver's side.

Oh, man.

There was a closed sign on the hardware store. He sure hadn't seen that when he'd stopped, but with Rayanne in tow, he ran toward a small newspaper office next door. Not his number-one choice of places to take cover since the front of the building was literally a wall of glass, but it beat going back into the street.

Maybe.

Perhaps it was the pain roaring through him, but he was getting plenty of mixed signals. One critical one, though. This didn't feel like a ruse.

It felt like yet another attempt to kill them.

"Get down!" he shouted to some men who were chatting just up the block. "Stay away from the truck!"

Hopefully, they'd listen and maybe it'd be enough to keep them and any other innocent bystanders out of harm's way. While he hoped, he added that this could just be a bad prank by kids with too much time on their hands.

Blue got Rayanne inside the office, and he pulled her to the floor next to the reception desk. No one was seated there, but it didn't take long before he heard footsteps running from the back. He levered up, took aim.

And got a shriek from the forty-something brunette woman who bolted toward them.

"Bomb threat," he warned her, and that got her running back up the hall. Good. Maybe she'd stay put.

Or not.

She kept going, straight out the back door. Blue hoped

there wasn't someone out there waiting, but at least the woman wasn't near the possible bomb.

Blue intended to get Rayanne away from the windows, as well, and back into one of the offices, but he had another look outside to make sure they wouldn't be gunned down the moment they stood.

And he saw something that caused the skin to crawl on the back of his neck.

There was a man on the opposite side of the street. He had on a nondescript brown delivery uniform and was standing by the side door of the antiques store. The guy was nondescript, too.

Well, except for the matching brown cap.

The man had it slung low so that it concealed part of his face. Again, it might be nothing, but Blue wasn't exactly in a trusting kind of mood.

"You recognize him?" Blue asked Rayanne.

She lifted her head just long enough to get a glimpse before Blue pushed her back down. "No. But I don't know many locals. Is he armed?"

"Could be. He has several boxes on a trolley, and they're blocking a good portion of his body." What the guy wasn't doing was looking their way.

That still didn't mean he wasn't a hired killer. He could just be watching to see what was going on.

"Come on," Blue insisted. "I need to get you away from this glass."

Rayanne didn't argue, but she also didn't have time to move before her phone rang.

Blue glanced at Cooper's name on the screen again. "We're in the newspaper office," he said the moment that Rayanne hit the answer button. "Please tell me this is all a hoax."

"Still trying to determine that," Cooper answered. "The bomb squad's on their way. Stay put until then."

He would, but he also kept his attention on the delivery man while he got Rayanne moving away from the window. Blue made sure she stayed low, and he kept himself in front of her in case this situation went from bad to worse.

"You're grunting," Rayanne whispered. "How bad is the pain?"

At the moment he hardly felt it, but Blue was sure it would hit him again when this was over. For now, he only wanted Rayanne safe.

They made it to the edge of the desk when Blue saw the delivery guy move. Not a slow, easy gesture, either. The man turned, leaving the boxes on the trolley, and he ran toward the back of the antiques store. Blue threw himself over Rayanne.

And not a second too soon.

The blast came.

It was deafening. A thundering ball of fire that hurled flames and debris in every direction, and it shook the entire building.

Including Rayanne and him.

This definitely hadn't been a ruse. That explosion was the real deal. The wall of glass shattered, and both the shards and the pieces of the truck slammed through what was left of the front of the office building.

Blue was instantly punched and pelted, but he forced himself to stay put. For several moments, anyway. Once he thought it might be the end of the flying debris, he got Rayanne moving into the hall so he could put some distance between her and anything else that might be about to come their way.

"That man could be coming," she said, her voice as shaky as the rest of her.

Yeah, and that was why he had to get her to safety.

Blue moved them up the hall to one of the offices, and he shoved Rayanne inside. She tried to pull him inside the room with her, but he stayed put.

And he took aim in case the killer was right on the heels of that explosion.

Still no sign of the delivery man, but it was chaos out there now. People shouting. Sirens blaring. Blue caught glimpses of people scattering to get away from those flames and a possible second explosion. Not that there'd been any indication of two bombs, but he wouldn't put it past the person who had orchestrated all of this.

Rayanne's phone rang again, and a moment later he heard her answer, "Cooper, we're okay. We're still in the newspaper office." She paused, punched the end-call button. "He says to wait here, that he's on the way."

Waiting sucked, but Blue knew it could have been a lot worse. If someone hadn't phoned in that bomb threat, then Rayanne and he would have been inside the truck when it turned into a fireball.

But who'd made that call to warn him?

Since the bomb hadn't been a hoax, maybe that meant someone close to the attacker didn't agree with this plan to kill Rayanne and him. Or maybe the explosion was meant for another reason. Perhaps just to torment and scare them.

If so, it'd worked.

Blue was scared, not for himself but for the hard-headed woman crouched next to him. Rayanne wasn't the backing-down sort, and she would try to go after this goon and get hurt. Or worse.

That took him right back to the theory that someone could be doing this to force Rayanne and him into what could end up being a failed attempt at some vigilante justice. Still, that didn't tell Blue who would do this or why.

"You're sure that Stetson and vest are lucky?" she grumbled.

Blue nearly laughed, *nearly*. Rayanne probably hadn't asked that to ease the tension, but it did just a little.

"We're still alive," he reminded her.

"Yeah, but if one more bad thing happens to us, I'm stripping them off you."

Again, she'd eased the tension, and embarrassed herself a little when she no doubt realized how that sounded. Blue could have dug himself a really big hole if he'd invited her to strip off his clothes anytime, anywhere. And that was an invitation he really wouldn't mind extending to her.

Rayanne's phone rang again, and this time she put it on speaker. "Colt's at the back door of the newspaper office," Cooper said. "He's got a truck that I want you and Blue to use to get to the ranch. I don't think it's a good idea for you to be in the middle of this."

Blue agreed, but his ATF training kicked in. "You might need help catching whoever did this."

"Yeah, but the best help you can give me now is to get my sister out of there."

Rayanne made a small sound. Not quite a huff but close enough. Probably because she was still at odds with Cooper and didn't appreciate him calling her *sister*. Or maybe she just didn't like being treated like a pregnant woman instead of a deputy sheriff.

Tough.

She was pregnant.

"I'll get her home," Blue assured Cooper. "Colt's cleared that back area?"

"As best he could. Just be careful."

Oh, Blue would.

They raced toward the back door, and the moment Blue eased it open and looked outside, he spotted Colt. The deputy had his gun ready, and he handed Blue the keys.

"The ranch hands know you're coming," Colt assured him. "They'll help you secure the place."

It wasn't as good as having armed, nonpregnant peace officers, but at least the ranch hands would be armed. Blue got her inside the truck, and he headed out.

He didn't have to remind Rayanne to keep watch. She did. She also kept her left hand positioned over her stomach. Not that he needed it, but it was yet another reminder of just how high the stakes were.

Thankfully, there weren't a lot of cars on the road leading out of town, and no one followed when he took the turn toward the ranch.

"I'm calling Seth," Rayanne said, still keeping watch. "I want him to make sure your boss gets that recording. The last thing we need right now is for him to arrest you."

She was right, but it surprised him that she'd remember to do something like this on the heels of the explosion.

"Gandy gave us a surveillance flash drive that clears Blue," Rayanne said when her brother answered. "I know you and Cooper can't stand the sight of each other, but you need to pick up the flash drive from the sheriff's office and get it to Agent Caleb Wiggs. We gave it to Cooper, but clearly he's got enough on his hands right now."

"Good day to you, too," Seth grumbled. "Are you all right?"

"What do you think? Someone just blew up my truck."

"I heard, and I'm repeating my question—are you all right?"

"I've been better," Rayanne said on a weary sigh. "Just please get the flash drive to Blue's boss."

"That explosion's given you a one-track mind, sis. Okay, I'll get the flash drive from Cooper—you'll owe me big-time for that—and I'll personally deliver it to Caleb Wiggs. In return, I want a favor from Blue."

"I'm listening," Blue said.

"Take care of my sister."

The look she shot Blue let him know that she wasn't happy about needing a babysitter, but then the look softened, and a sigh left her mouth. Maybe she'd resigned herself to the fact that Blue was going to be around a lot longer than she'd wanted him to be.

Blue thanked Seth, ended the call and took the final turn to the ranch. There were no vehicles on the road, but there was a black truck parked at the end of the cattle gate.

"What the heck?" Rayanne mumbled, moving to the edge of the seat.

Blue wanted to know the same thing.

There was a man and a woman standing outside the truck, and they darn sure weren't alone. There were four ranch hands standing between the couple and the road, and each hand had a gun pointed at their visitors.

Blue slowed to a crawl, but he got close enough to get a better look at the man. At first he thought it was Gandy making a return visit.

But it wasn't Gandy.

This man had his arms folded over his chest, clearly waiting.

"Is that who I think it is?" Blue asked.

"Yes." Rayanne pulled in a hard breath. "It's Wendell Braddock."

Chapter Nine

Even on a good day, Rayanne wouldn't have offered Wendell a friendly greeting, and today certainly didn't qualify as good. Well, other than the fact that Blue and she had managed to survive yet another attack and were still alive, but the sound of that blast was too fresh in her ears to play nice with a man who might want her dead.

Might.

Of course, Gandy could have made it look as if Wendell was the bad guy. Gandy had certainly had enough practice doing bad-guy stuff. It didn't mean Rayanne intended to trust Wendell or any other member of the Braddock clan.

"I'll handle this," Blue insisted. "Wait here." He brought the truck to a stop and would have bolted out if Rayanne hadn't taken him by the wrist.

She was about to tell him that he was in no shape to battle anyone. However, she had to reassess that when she studied his face. Blue probably was still in pain and weak from the surgery, but he sure didn't look it.

"You look mad enough to rip off Wendell's head," she warned him. "If he's behind these attacks, I wouldn't mind you doing that, but if he's not, it'll be hard for him to give us any answers if you beat him senseless."

Blue didn't jump to agree with her. He sat there for a moment, obviously trying to rein in his temper. The sound of the explosion was no doubt too fresh in his head, as well.

He finally nodded, got out and then shot her a scowl when she followed him. Rayanne slid across the seat and got out on the driver's side so that she'd be next to Blue.

"A little bird told me about the trouble you've been having lately," Wendell greeted. He looked and sounded about as friendly to them as Rayanne felt about him. "Also heard that you might be looking to pin that trouble on me."

"I'd love to do that," Rayanne greeted right back. "Why? Are you here to confess?"

"He most certainly is not," the woman next to him said. "What he should do is go home and let his lawyers deal with this."

Wendell smiled, not exactly in a happy way but more like a man who was trying to placate the woman. "This is my assistant, Ruby-Lee Evans."

"I'm his nurse," she crisply corrected. "And I'm his friend. He had a bad spell with his heart just last week and he's not thinking straight. He shouldn't be putting himself through this kind of stress."

Rayanne didn't know the dynamics of what was going on here, but Wendell was a widower, so it was possible Ruby-Lee was more than just an assistant, nurse and friend.

"I'm not gonna last much longer," Wendell added, his gaze shifting back to Rayanne. "But it'd better be long enough for me to see your murdering mother get what she deserves. And what she deserves is a needle in her arm."

Rayanne had expected that attitude. Heck, half the

town felt the same way. But it cut her to the core that her mother could actually be convicted and given the death penalty for a crime that Rayanne was certain she hadn't committed. Of course, the Braddocks were equally certain that she had.

"Is that what the attacks on Rayanne are about?" Blue asked. "You're trying to give Jewell McKinnon what you think she deserves?"

For several moments, Wendell didn't say or do anything, but then he shook his head. "I'd love nothing more than to see that witch Jewell suffer by losing a kid or two. Then she'd know what it was like for me to lose Whitt. But, no, I didn't put a hit on Rayanne."

"You're sure about that?" Rayanne pressed. "Because a little bird told me that you'd met with the very man who tried to kill Blue and me. That same little bird said there was proof—a photograph."

"I meet with a lot of people," Wendell answered. "But I don't meet with hired killers. I don't have so much as a parking ticket, much less contact with felons."

"Are you saying the photo was doctored?" Rayanne snapped.

"I'm saying if I met with somebody like that, then I wouldn't have known who he really was. Somebody's setting me up."

Blue huffed. "And who would do that to a kindly old man like you?"

Wendell shrugged, obviously not offended by his sarcasm. "Rex Gandy. I heard he wasn't happy when he found out you were an undercover ATF agent who'd been digging into his business and that Rayanne here helped you out with that digging."

"His *illegal arms* business," Rayanne corrected in case

Wendell didn't know just how dirty Gandy was. However, she was betting that Wendell did know. The man seemed to be well-informed about all of this.

"Why would Gandy come after Blue and me now?" she came out and asked. Maybe, just maybe, she'd get a truthful answer.

"I don't know for sure, but if I had to venture a guess, I'd say it's because he figured out that Agent McCurdy here was alive and well. Or maybe I should say alive and dirty." Wendell smiled again. "It doesn't bother you, girl, that your man was hired to kill you?"

"A lot of things bother me," she settled for saying.

It concerned her more that Wendell had details that he had likely gotten from Gandy. She didn't want these two snakes teaming up against Blue and her.

But maybe they already had.

Blue and she exchanged glances, and she saw in his eyes that he'd come to that same conclusion. If so, it was an unholy alliance with plenty of money and just as much motive. Both men could want revenge against Blue and her.

"So why are you here?" Blue asked Wendell. "To warn us about Gandy?" He didn't wait for the man to answer. "Because we already knew he was a dirtbag. The question is, are you a dirtbag, too?"

That clearly didn't please Ruby-Lee. She mumbled something about leaving and tried to get Wendell back in his truck. The man shook off her grip.

"I'm a still-grieving father who lost his son because of her mother." Wendell tipped his head to Rayanne. "I don't care what happens to either of you, but I want my name kept out of this. I don't want Rayanne or you or her badge-wearing brothers to try to muddy the waters of her mother's trial by saying I tried to kill you."

And it would indeed muddy the waters.

So much so that her mother's attorney could ask for not just a change of venue but perhaps a mistrial since it'd been the Braddocks who'd pushed for Jewell's arrest. So Wendell had a good reason to have his name not associated with any harm that might come Rayanne and her siblings' way.

Still, that didn't mean Wendell was innocent.

"Maybe you believe you can have your cake and eat it, too," Rayanne suggested. "You could get revenge against Jewell by killing one of her kids and then placing the blame on somebody else."

Wendell certainly didn't deny it with words, but that sent a flash of anger through his eyes. "You're barking up the wrong tree, little girl. Keep doing it, and you might just get hurt."

Wendell turned, and Ruby-Lee and he got back in his truck. Rayanne wanted to grab him, haul him to the sheriff's office and force him to say more.

But he wouldn't.

Wendell would just hide behind his lawyers and claim the McKinnons were harassing him. What she needed was proof, even if that proof cleared Wendell's name.

"You need to be looking at Gandy," Wendell said, speaking through the rolled-down window. "Or somebody else," he added, and he looked straight at Blue.

Because her arm was right against Blue's, she felt his muscles stiffen. "I'm not behind these attacks, so you'd better not mean me by that *somebody else*."

Wendell shook his head. "Just repeating more little-bird talk. I figure once your head heals, you could remember all sorts of things that a certain person might not want you to remember."

"What person?" Blue snapped. "You?"

Wendell smiled a syrupy-sweet smile that no one could have mistaken as genuine. "No, Caleb Wiggs, your boss."

BLUE MADE THE CALL to Caleb the moment he got Rayanne inside the ranch house. But he cursed when his call went straight to voice mail. He wanted answers *now,* but obviously he was going to have to wait. Blue left a message to phone him back ASAP, and that wait had better not be too long.

"Stating the obvious here," Rayanne said, "but Wendell could be lying."

Yeah, Blue knew that, but until he heard that from Caleb, it wouldn't sit easy in his mind. Why the heck would a man like Wendell even sling an accusation like that when he must have known that Blue could easily find out he was lying?

Well, he could if Caleb would answer his bloomin' phone.

"Have there been any hints that Caleb's dirty?" Rayanne asked.

"None." But he had to shake his head. "I don't remember any."

So why did he have this nagging feeling that there was something to remember? Something caught in that whirl of details still inside his head? Blue hated to have doubts, but they came. Man, did they.

"Sit," Rayanne insisted, practically putting him onto the sofa in the family room. For a moment he thought she'd done that because he looked ready to explode, but she eased his vest and shirt off his injured shoulder and checked the bandage.

"I'm fine." Blue nearly pulled away from her but then quickly figured out that he liked Rayanne fussing over him. Even if she was scowling when she did it.

"At least you didn't pop your stitches this time." Rayanne put his clothes back in place, and in the process her fingers brushed over the left side of his leather vest. She pulled her hand away, but she looked at the spot where she'd likely felt the slight indentations caused by pinholes.

They were still there after all these years.

"I don't remember you ever wearing your badge on this vest," she pointed out.

"No." And because he didn't want her to move away from him, he said something that he hoped would make her stay. "But there was a badge on it a long time ago. My dad's."

Well, she didn't move. Probably because he'd never before mentioned his father to her. Come to think of it, he hadn't mentioned him to anyone since he was a kid. It was part of that baggage that he'd always sworn he wouldn't discuss.

"He was a cop?" she asked.

Blue nodded. "A small-town deputy sheriff."

Like Rayanne. That tightened his gut a bit because he wanted things to turn out a lot better for her than they had for his dad.

She opened her mouth, met his gaze for just a second, and with just that glance, he could practically see the wheels turning in her troubled head. Rayanne was still trying to keep him at arm's length, but a personal conversation like this had a way of pulling a person closer, not pushing him away. She knew that as well as Blue did.

"It's none of my business," she said. Rayanne would have gotten up, too, if Blue hadn't taken her hand.

"Maybe not, but since that's my baby you're carrying, if anybody's got a right to know, it's you."

That didn't help the scowl, but she didn't knock his hand away. "We agreed we weren't going to talk about this yet."

Not really. She'd laid down the law, and he'd had too many other things on his mind—like keeping her alive—to argue with her. Blue didn't want to argue with her now, but with Rayanne this close to him, those memories were starting to stir again.

The kiss in the hospital.

And before that, before that rock had crashed into his head, there'd been some scalding-hot looks between Rayanne and him. They'd both had enough sense not to act on that heat, because work and sex rarely mixed.

Well, except for the one night.

Blue figured it'd been a pretty good mix.

He reached out and slid a strand of hair off her cheek and back in the direction of her ponytail. "I wish I could remember sleeping with you."

"I wish you'd quit talking about it," she fired back.

Yeah, that was his Rayanne. She could get testy if you weren't on her side, and she probably wasn't sure if she could fully trust him yet.

She could.

But that kind of trust had to be earned, and it wouldn't help matters if the heat got all mixed up in this again.

"I might just kick you six ways to Sunday if you try to kiss me again," she warned him.

"It'd be worth it," he mumbled.

That put some more annoyance in her eyes, but she stayed put as if steeling herself to weather a mighty storm.

Blue eased his hand onto her shoulder, then to the back of her head. He slipped his fingers in her hair and gave Rayanne a chance to settle and go still. He also kept an eye on her knee. She wouldn't actually try to hurt him— well, maybe not, anyway—but he didn't want her using that knee to try to get her point across.

Besides, he already knew this was a mistake.

The mistake went full-blown when he touched his mouth to hers. He felt the jolt just as he had in the hospital. Felt the heat, too.

She shook her head, maybe trying to clear it, but she didn't back away. Instead Rayanne cursed him.

Then kissed him right back.

Another jolt. It was a nice one that slipped through his body and settled right behind the zipper of his jeans. He kept things gentle. At first. But with each movement of their mouths, each shift of the pressure, the heat went from a simmer to a full flame.

"You taste good," he whispered against her mouth.

"You taste bad," she answered.

He pulled back, met her eye to eye. His eyebrow rose a fraction.

"You always were the bad boy," Rayanne explained. "And I don't want you to taste good. Or smell good. Or feel good." She cursed him again and gave his hand a slight squeeze before she looked away. "But you do, and that makes you bad."

Sadly, he knew exactly what she meant. Did that stop him?

No.

"This would be so much easier if I didn't remember

the attraction," he told her. "I could focus just on making sure you and the baby are safe. Yeah, I know," he added before Rayanne could dole out another warning about that. "A conversation about the baby's off-limits."

She stood, her back to him now. "Once your memory returns, then you'll know more of how you feel about what happened between us."

Okay, now he was confused. "Are we talking about sex?"

Rayanne didn't jump to answer, but after several long moments, she nodded. "Sure."

Which was probably female code for *you idiot, we're not talking about sex.*

Blue stood, fully intending to admit his idiocy—embrace it, even—and insist on the heart-to-heart that Rayanne clearly wanted to avoid. However, his phone rang before he could even get the conversation started. Huffing, he glanced at the screen, figuring it was Caleb ready to give Blue some much-needed answers.

But *Unknown Caller* popped up on the screen.

He hit the answer button and put the call on speaker. "Agent McCurdy," he answered.

"Blue," the man said. His voice was a husky whisper, mostly breath. "This is Woody Janson."

Woody, his missing friend and former partner at the ATF. "Where are you?"

"Someplace safe. I can't say the same for you, Blue. You're in deep trouble. Rayanne, too."

"Yeah, someone's trying to kill us. What do you know about that?"

"Everything," Woody answered. "God, Blue. I'm so sorry."

Chapter Ten

Rayanne held her breath, hoping that Woody would just blurt out everything he knew. Not only about the attacks but also about why Blue had gone missing in the first place. However, Woody didn't.

"I have to go," Woody said instead. "But we need to meet right away."

Of course he would say that, and Blue shook his head before the man even finished. "I'm not leaving Rayanne, and I don't want to take her off the ranch. Just tell me what you know."

"I can't get into it all over the phone. Someone might be listening. I'll send you a text with a meeting place and time." With that, Woody hung up.

Blue cursed, groaned and tried to call the man back, but he didn't get an answer. However, he did get a text within just a few seconds. One that obviously confused him, because he held up the screen for her to see the address.

Now she groaned. "It's a house on the ranch, about a quarter of a mile from here. It used to belong to my grandfather, but when he passed away, he left it to my brother Tucker. He lives there now."

Blue stayed quiet a moment, obviously giving that

some thought. "He's the one who's a Texas Ranger. You think he knows Woody?"

"Maybe, but Tucker's not there and hasn't been for a couple of days. He and his fiancée are in San Antonio trying to expedite the paperwork for the twin babies they're adopting."

Just to be sure that Tucker hadn't returned, Rayanne tried to call his house phone but as expected, she got no answer. "When does Woody want to meet?"

"In thirty minutes."

So soon. Rayanne heard the concern in his voice, the same concern flashing in her head like a neon sign. Danger. But was the danger worth learning what Woody might know?

Everything, the man had said.

"Can we really afford not to hear what he knows?" Rayanne asked.

Again, he started shaking his head. "I'm not putting you in danger again."

"Maybe the danger's already right here. You heard what he said about you and me not being in a safe place. If there's something going on, I want to know what it is so we can stop it."

"Yeah," he mumbled, but he didn't sound convinced.

"You could text him back and tell him to come here instead."

More head shaking. "I don't want him inside."

"Then we'll talk to him on the back porch with the ranch hands standing guard. If he tries to bring anyone else with him, we'll know and nix the meeting."

Still he didn't jump to agree, but his jaw was flexing. "You won't be with me while I talk with him."

Because she wanted to hear what Woody had to say,

Rayanne considered arguing, but she felt a strange flutter in her stomach. Like butterflies flapping their wings. The timing was certainly odd—and a little eerie, too—but she was certain this was the baby.

A first, though the doctor had said she would feel "quickening" around twenty weeks, and that was exactly how far along she was.

Blue practically jumped to his feet. "Are you okay?"

"I'm fine. The baby just moved, that's all."

Her words were meant to assure him that she wasn't in pain or anything, but those little flutters were one of the most important things that she'd ever experienced.

Blue pressed his hand on her stomach, but the fluttering stopped. She wasn't sure who seemed more disappointed about that—him or her. Rayanne hadn't expected to want to share this with anyone, including Blue, but she found herself wanting to do just that.

"The text," she reminded him, stepping back so that his hand was no longer on her stomach.

Yes, it was a special moment, but distractions like that could get them killed, or at least prevent them from getting the information to put an end to the danger.

Blue glanced down at her stomach, then the phone, and after mumbling something, he sent the text to Woody switching the location to the back porch. The moment that Blue got a confirmation text back from the man, Rayanne called one of the top ranch hands, Arlene, and told her about their visitor who'd be arriving shortly. She asked Arlene to make arrangements for some security.

And for Woody to be frisked for weapons.

It might be overkill, but after everything that'd happened, Rayanne wasn't taking any chances.

"Is it possible to sneak up on the house from the back?" Blue asked the moment she was done.

"Maybe," she had to admit. "There are acres of pasture, some with trees and rocks like the place where those other men attacked us."

That got his jaw muscles working again. "You *will* stay inside." He waited until she nodded. Waited even longer until she actually said "Yes" before they started toward the back of the house.

They'd made it only a few steps when Blue's phone rang, and Rayanne held her breath while he checked the screen. She hoped Woody hadn't already changed his mind about this meeting. Hoped even more that nothing else had gone wrong.

"It's Clifford Hale, Caleb's boss," Blue said, and he hit the speaker button. "Agent McCurdy."

"Blue," the man said, his voice all business. "Where the hell is Caleb?"

"I don't know. I was about to ask you the same thing. He's not answering his phone or returning my calls. What's going on?"

"Well, it's not good, and he needs to come in and answer some questions."

Blue huffed. "Questions about me?"

"Yes, and his possible involvement with one of the suspects in your shooting. Rex Gandy."

Gandy again. She hated how his name kept popping up, and she nearly blurted out some questions for Hale, but Rayanne figured those questions would be better coming from Blue, one of Hale's fellow agents.

"Possible involvement?" Blue repeated. "You got any evidence?"

"I got squat, other than a questionable tip from an

equally questionable criminal informant who wants to be paid and could be yapping his trap just for the money."

"Is it the same one who claimed I'd been hired as a hit man?" Blue pressed.

Hale hesitated, probably because he was trying to figure out how much to tell him. "Yeah, the same one. But I'm sure Caleb could clear all of this up if he'd just get his butt back in here and start talking."

Rayanne hoped that was true. Not just for Caleb but for Blue and Woody, as well.

She waited to see if Blue was going to mention the meeting with Woody, but he saw her eyeing him and must have guessed what she had on her mind, because he shook his head.

"Speaking of clearing things up," Blue said to Hale, "I'm not guilty of trying to kill Rayanne McKinnon. There's a lot of crazy stuff going on—"

"I know," Hale interrupted. "I just got off the phone with Sheriff Cooper McKinnon, and he filled me in. Don't worry. He's working on it and so are the FBI and the ATF. Me included. The pictures and flash drive that Gandy gave him have already been sent to the lab for analysis—"

"That's a start," Blue interrupted right back, "but I got a visit earlier from a man in one of those photos, Wendell Braddock. He implied that Caleb's dirty and wants me dead because of something I might remember once I recover from this concussion. Is any part of that true?"

Rayanne didn't like the long silence that followed.

No. Not this. There were already too many people they couldn't trust without adding lawmen to the mix.

"Like I said, I'm working on it. If Caleb contacts you, have him call me immediately. And if he doesn't, I want his badge. *Tell him.*" With that barked order, Hale ended the call, leaving Blue and her staring at each other.

It sickened her to think of Caleb as a suspect, especially after the way he'd acted in the hospital. All concerned about Blue's well-being. But just minutes after that concern, the gunmen had shown up to attack them.

Was it possible that Caleb had orchestrated that?

"Well, I guess this means I won't be arrested," Blue mumbled, sliding his phone into his pocket.

That was something at least, but they needed a lot more things to go right. Like getting information that actually made sense.

"How would Wendell have found out about all of this?" she asked.

Blue shook his head. "Maybe from Gandy? I doubt they're friends, but Gandy could have just called him. Unless there's a leak in the sheriff's office?"

"Not likely. Cooper might be pigheaded and blind when it comes to our mother's innocence, but he runs a tight department. He wouldn't have anyone working for him that he didn't trust." She paused, thought about it. "But Gandy would have almost certainly called Wendell if he thought Wendell could make our lives more difficult."

Or put them in more danger.

"If Gandy's behind the failed attacks, then maybe he thought he'd be able to spur Wendell into killing us," Blue suggested.

Her pulse was already thick and throbbing, and Blue's words didn't help steady it any. As a deputy, she was accustomed to people wanting to harm her, but that was only while they were in the commission of a crime. This was, well, more personal, and because of the baby, the stakes were higher than they'd ever been.

"Your visitor's here," Arlene called out from the back of the house.

When Blue and Rayanne made it to the door, they found the woman standing guard there. Rayanne also spotted the tall, lanky man making his way along the side of the house. Not alone. There were two armed ranch hands trailing along behind him.

Blue gave her one last reminder to stay put, and he walked out onto the porch, which stretched across the back of the house. Rayanne stayed at the glass-front door and watched the man come up the steps. She'd never seen Woody before, but she didn't have to know the man to see the fear in his eyes and the vigilance in his body language.

Woody wasn't any more comfortable with this visit than they were.

"How'd you get here?" Blue came right out and asked.

Woody hitched his thumb in the direction of the road. "I hid my car behind some trees and walked. I don't think anyone followed me, but if someone gets close to my car, I'll get an alert on my phone."

A phone that he had clutched in his hand like a weapon. One of the ranch hands was holding a Glock, no doubt Woody's, probably taken when he searched him.

Woody looked at the bruise on Blue's head and cursed. "How close did you come to getting killed?"

"Close," Blue readily answered. "And because of this lump on my head, I've got some gaps in my memory. You said you knew *everything,* so start from the beginning. Tell me what happened that put Rayanne and me into this mess."

Woody pulled in a long breath, cast an uneasy glance around him. A cop's glance. "Five months ago I was deep undercover in a militia group, and I overheard a conversation between two thugs who said that they'd been hired to stop you."

"Stop me why?" Blue immediately asked.

Woody shook his head. "They were vague about it, but I gathered that you'd gotten too close in an investigation."

"Gandy," Rayanne mumbled.

Woody looked over Blue's shoulder at her and nodded. "That was my guess, too. But these men hadn't been hired to kill Blue. They were going to kidnap both of you and then torture Rayanne until Blue agreed to fix the investigation."

Rayanne eased her hand to the doorjamb to steady herself. She hated such a wimpy reaction, but it wasn't every day that she heard of plans to torture her.

"Why go after me to get to Blue?" she asked.

"They'd been watching him and knew that you two had spent the night together. I guess they figured you meant a lot to Blue." Woody's attention shifted back to Blue. "I sneaked away from the group as soon as I could and called you."

"A conversation that I only vaguely remember," Blue said. "What'd you tell me?"

"That you were both in danger and that if you hurried, you might have time to catch these guys before they got close enough to carry out their plan. I gave you their location, and you said you would arrange for someone to guard Rayanne before you left and went after them."

Blue looked back at her, probably to see how she was handling all of this. She tried to look strong, but Rayanne was certain she failed miserably. He'd left to try to save her.

And it had worked.

Well, until now, that is.

"While I was on the phone with you," Woody continued, "I realized someone was listening in on our conversation. It was one of the members of the militia group that I'd infiltrated. I hung up, and he took a shot at me. I barely managed to get out of there, and I went on the run."

Well, that explained Woody's disappearance. In part, anyway.

"Why not run to the ATF?" Blue asked him.

"Because those two thugs had personal info about you. The kind of info they could only get from classified files at the Justice Department. I figured there was a mole in the ATF, and I wanted to do some investigating before I went waltzing into a trap that could get me killed."

Judging from the way Woody kept looking around, he still thought being killed was a possibility. It was. He was in danger just by being around them.

"I haven't found proof of a mole," Woody continued a moment later, "but I've heard bad buzz about Caleb."

Blue nodded. "So have I. Is he dirty, or is someone setting him up like they did me?"

Woody lifted his shoulder. "Some guns recently surfaced that you had confiscated in a raid earlier this year. Well, according to your report, you had. Caleb claims he didn't know anything about it, and he has no idea how the guns got back in the hands of some drug runners. Since you were presumed dead, you weren't around to answer questions about it."

"I did confiscate weapons," Blue verified. He touched his fingers to his head as if trying to draw out the details.

"I told you about them, and my report would have gone directly to Caleb. It's possible he didn't read it. Or remember it. But it was a big cache."

"Is that why Caleb's under investigation?" Rayanne asked Woody. "Because of those weapons?"

"That's part of it, but the buzz also points to something else." Again, Woody's attention landed on her. "There's a criminal informant, Lennie Sunderland, who's clamoring that Caleb wants you both dead because now that Blue's back, he could have told you about those missing weapons."

Well, they finally had a name to the rather chatty CI who was slinging accusations right and left. "Blue didn't tell me anything about weapons."

"You're positive?" Woody pressed.

While nothing about this visit had exactly made her comfortable, that put her on full alert. Because Woody could be the person behind the attacks, and hiding the chain-of-custody trail on those weapons could be his motive. Of course, the others—Wendell, Gandy and maybe even Caleb—apparently had motives, too.

Caleb could be trying to cover up his own crime.

"I'm positive Blue didn't tell me," Rayanne assured the man, and she remembered every detail of the night that'd changed her life in both good and bad ways.

"Why'd I fake my death?" Blue asked Woody.

"I don't know for sure. In fact, I thought you really were dead. But in light of everything that's happened, I can guess that when you didn't catch the men hired to kidnap and kill you and Rayanne, you thought *dying* was the best way to keep her safe. And it worked until someone found out you were alive."

Blue cursed. "I shouldn't have come here. I brought the killers to her."

That wasn't easy to hear, either, and Rayanne reminded herself that there had to be more to it than that.

"I don't think you had a choice but to come here," Woody insisted. "Someone found out you were alive, and I'm sure it didn't take long for word to spread to the wrong people." Woody paused. "God, I'm so sorry, Blue, but I might be the reason word got out."

Even though she couldn't see Blue's face, she saw the change in his body language. "What do you mean?" he asked.

Woody wearily shook his head. "I was looking for a way to eliminate the militia so that I wouldn't have to stay in hiding. I needed access to some information through some of our old contacts, and I used one of your aliases."

Rayanne's stomach knotted. She'd worked with the ATF enough to know that while in deep cover, agents sometimes used not only identities but code words set up by the criminals. Code words that told the thugs and gunrunners they could trust this person. When Woody used Blue's alias and code words, then those thugs would have believed it was Blue himself using them.

"I honestly thought you were dead," Woody repeated.

Blue groaned and looked back at her, and in his eyes, she could see the apology. An unnecessary one and one he didn't get a chance to voice aloud, because Woody's phone beeped.

The man hadn't exactly been at ease during any part of this visit, but the small sound put him on alert.

"Someone's near my car," Woody mumbled, his attention zooming to his phone screen. "I have it rigged with security cameras." He pressed some buttons, and Blue moved closer to have a look, as well.

Both Woody and Blue cursed.

"You recognize him?" Woody asked.

"Yeah." Blue took the phone and held it up for her to see the man prowling around the car. He was armed with a rifle with a long-range scope, and there was another gun tucked in a shoulder holster.

"That's the hired gun who came to the ranch yesterday to kill us. He's the one who escaped." Rayanne tried not to shudder. "Where exactly are you parked?"

"Too close. By your brother's house."

Oh, mercy. He was right. That was too close. Especially since the gunman had that rifle. He was already in range of the ranch house.

"Get Rayanne away from the doors and windows," Woody told Blue. "And no one's to follow me. Too dangerous." He snatched his Glock from the ranch hand and bolted off the porch.

Woody hit the ground running.

Chapter Eleven

Blue was thankful for everything Woody had just told him, but he hoped they hadn't gotten that information at a sky-high price—another attack.

"Set the security alarm," he told Rayanne.

His gun was already drawn, and Blue locked up. He did the same to the front door, and then Rayanne and he raced upstairs to the guest room where he'd been staying.

There were still plenty of windows in the room, but he didn't want her downstairs in case the thug tried to break in and started shooting. This way, the guy would have to make it up the stairs to have a chance of getting to her.

Blue would stop him before that happened.

"Stay down," he warned her. "And call one of your brothers for backup."

While Rayanne made the call, Blue hurried to the window that would give him the best vantage point to see if the assassin was coming after them. Well, it would if the guy came to the house and took a direct route to get there. It was possible that he'd try to sneak closer to the ranch house some other way.

"Colt's already on the way. Arlene called him." Rayanne sank down onto the floor, her back against the door. "Do you see Woody and the other man?"

"No. I don't even see his car." Of course, Woody had mentioned that he'd parked near some trees, so the vehicle could possibly be hidden.

"You believe everything Woody said?" Rayanne asked a moment later.

Blue had already given that some thought during their conversation. "I can't think of a reason he'd lie…unless he's the one trying to kill us."

She made a sound of agreement. "He could have said those things about Caleb to make him look guilty. Of course, Caleb's own behavior doesn't help matters, since he's not around to defend himself."

No, it didn't help, and that was even more reason for Blue to find Caleb and talk to him. However, he didn't want to do that by putting Rayanne at further risk.

While he kept watch, he tried to force the memories to come. And some did. Fragments of his conversations with Woody. Some images of him leaving Rayanne asleep in bed after they'd made love. Even a few bits and pieces of him going after those men who'd planned to kidnap and kill Rayanne and him.

Nothing in those fragments led him to believe the man was lying.

"You faked your death to save me," Rayanne said almost in a whisper. "I need to thank you for that."

She still didn't sound pleased that he'd taken such measures to protect her, but Blue wasn't about to apologize for it. It'd kept her alive.

The baby, too.

And because he'd done such a good job of faking his death, it had prompted Woody to use an identity that had ultimately gotten the wrong person's attention.

But who was the wrong person?

"I'm remembering some stuff," he told her.

Rayanne stayed quiet a moment. "*Stuff* about us?"

"Some."

"Some?" she repeated in a mumble, and then added a little *hmmp* sound. "You've been on the run for nearly five months, and it's possible you've gotten involved with someone else."

Ah, so that was the reason for her mumble of disapproval. "No memories of that, and I suspect getting involved with another woman was the last thing on my mind."

Especially after he'd been with Rayanne.

That thought didn't exactly please him. He didn't need his full memory to know that he wasn't the sort for a permanent relationship, but that had to change now. The baby made this permanent, and while that wouldn't please Rayanne, Blue didn't want an out when it came to his child.

His phone rang, and without taking his attention from the window, he hit the button to put the call on speaker. Blue had hoped it was an update from Woody, saying he'd caught the assassin, but it wasn't Woody's voice that poured through the room.

"This is Wendell Braddock," the caller said. "Did I call at a bad time?"

Blue couldn't tell if the man's dripping sarcasm was directed at their current situation or just at this whole mess in general.

"I'm busy," Blue snapped. "What'd you want?"

"Just heard about that photo of me that you got from Gandy. It was altered. I didn't meet with any hit man, but someone obviously wanted to make it look as if I did."

Blue wouldn't believe that until he heard it from the

lab or Rayanne's brother, but it did make him wonder. "How'd you find out so fast?"

"I have connections here and there," Wendell readily admitted.

That definitely didn't ease Blue's doubts about the man. Plus, the timing of the call was suspicious, and Wendell could have made it just to distract him.

"Somebody doctored that picture so we'd be at each other's throats," Wendell went on. "That way, he'll have a better shot at killing you."

"Yeah, yeah."

Blue had already figured out that potential angle, and he hit the end-call button, hanging up on him. It'd likely rile a man who was already riled, but it was better than Blue losing focus with a call that could wait.

Even if there was nothing to see.

Not Woody and not that hired killer.

But in the distance he heard a siren. Colt. Maybe if Woody needed help, Colt would get to him in time. Blue hated that he couldn't be out there himself, but he wasn't about to leave Rayanne unprotected.

Blue held his breath and tried to listen over the sound of his own pulse.

Had he heard some kind of popping sound?

Maybe.

But if so, it definitely wasn't a gunshot. Not a regular one, anyway, but it was possible a shot had been fired from a gun fitted with a silencer. Or maybe it was just his imagination galloping out of control.

He was so focused on trying to figure out what it was that the next sound nearly caused him to jump out of his skin. Hardly a manly reaction.

The ringing echoed through the room. Not Blue's

phone but Rayanne's, and he figured it was Wendell calling to whine about Blue having hung up on him.

But it wasn't.

"It's my mother," she said, and she let the call keep ringing until it went to voice mail. "If I talk to her now, she'll hear the concern in my voice, and it'll cause her to worry."

That must have been a big no-no for Rayanne since her mother had to be calling from the county jail, where she was being held without bond. Prisoners didn't get to make personal calls whenever it suited them, and this was probably the only call of the day or maybe even the week that Jewell would be granted.

The siren came closer, and Blue spotted Colt pulling to a stop near the white house where Woody had said he'd parked. Despite the fact there were now two ranch hands in place to give him backup, Colt didn't get out right away. Several moments later Blue's phone dinged.

No sign of Woody or the hired gun, Colt texted.

Heck. That wasn't what Blue wanted to hear. He wanted the assassin arrested and locked away so he couldn't attack again. It also would have been nice to question Woody some more, too.

A car's here, Colt added. I'll look around.

Blue relayed the texts to Rayanne and continued to keep watch.

From the corner of his eye, he saw Rayanne push the voice-mail button on her phone, and even though the sound was obviously turned down, Blue still heard her mother.

"I'm sorry you didn't answer, Rayanne." Jewell's voice was soft. Soothing, even. "I just wanted to check and see how you were. Are you taking care of yourself?"

Blue got another flash of memories. Of Rayanne in the back pasture when she came to his aid. And when she'd put her own life in danger.

No, she hadn't been taking care of herself.

She'd saved him.

"Your sister visited me this morning," Jewell went on. "She brought Seth with her. They wouldn't admit it, but I could tell he was there to protect her. Rosalie said Blue had come back and was staying at the ranch...."

Well, that would have been an interesting conversation. Since Jewell didn't know the reason he'd walked out on her daughter and now had put both Rosalie and her in danger, Jewell was likely one upset mama.

"Soon maybe you can tell me how you feel about Blue's return," Jewell continued. "*Or not.* I doubt you'll want to talk about him, but here's some motherly advice. Forgiveness is good for the soul and the heart. I love you, Rayanne. We'll talk soon."

So, not a riled mama protecting her baby girl. Blue expected Rayanne to dismiss that "motherly advice" in some way, but instead he heard a sound that he darn sure hadn't expected to hear.

"You're crying?" he asked when he heard the distinctive sniffs.

Blue glanced at her again and saw her quickly wipe away the tears. "It's hormones. They've got my emotions out of whack."

Because Blue considered himself a smart man, he didn't challenge that, though he wished he could go to Rayanne and pull her into his arms. He'd known her a couple of years now and had never seen her close to crying. Maybe hormones had something to do with it, but he figured the main reason was the stress over her mother's situation.

And their own.

"There are only four people I'd take a bullet for," Rayanne added in a mumble, "and my mother's one of them."

"Who are the other three?" he automatically asked. Why, he didn't know. Wait, yeah, he did. He wanted to hear Rayanne say who exactly was important to her.

She paused so long that he wasn't sure she'd actually answer. "Rosalie, Seth and now the baby."

"Wait." Now it was his turn to pause. "I've heard you say that before. Before I left, I mean, and before you were pregnant. You didn't say the baby then—"

"Because I had no idea that I was pregnant when you left." She stood, and after another glimpse of her expression, Blue knew that she expected this conversation to end.

It didn't end, though.

Rayanne tilted her head to the side. "Just how much of your memory are you getting back, anyway?"

"Some things." And some of those things he wouldn't share with her. No reason for her to relive the shooting here at the ranch when her memories were no doubt way too fresh. "It's nowhere near complete. More like flashes of images, sounds…scents."

Her eyebrow rose. "Scents?"

"Of you mostly and that night we were together before I left. You smelled like cinnamon."

She looked away, and Blue figured that was a good time to get his attention firmly back on the window.

"I'd had a cinnamon latte," she confirmed. "You remember our conversation?" Rayanne added that last part tentatively, like a woman walking on eggshells.

Again, he remembered only parts of the chat they'd had, and Blue pressed himself for more, hoping his brain would cooperate. However, before that could happen, his phone rang, and he saw Colt's name on the screen. Blue put the call on speaker, hoping this wasn't another dose of bad news.

"Still no sign of either of them," Colt explained. "You're sure Woody was headed this way when he left the ranch house?"

"Not positive. He could have gone elsewhere. I lost sight of him for about five minutes or so while I was getting Rayanne to safety."

"So she's okay, then," Colt said, sounding very much like a brother.

"Yeah," Blue verified. For now. He needed to keep it that way.

"Well, Woody's car is empty and completely clean inside," Colt continued a moment later. "From the looks of it, the steering wheel and gear stick have been wiped down. Nothing in the glove compartment. There's not even a scrap of paper or debris on the floor. I phoned in the license plate, and it's bogus."

Probably because Woody hadn't wanted the vehicle traced to him. He was an ATF agent, after all, and knew the tricks to staying hidden.

"Then how did the assassin find Woody?" Blue asked, more to himself than Colt.

"Hard to say. The ranch hands and I are following the tracks now, and it appears the gunman came in from the main road. Probably walked here, because I don't see evidence of a second vehicle. That could mean he had Woody under surveillance."

Yeah, or else the guy had managed to put a tracking

device on the car. But the assassin didn't need a track-ing device or surveillance for that. If Jewell knew about Blue being at the ranch with Rayanne, then it was likely all over town.

So maybe the gunman was solely after Woody this time instead of Rayanne and him?

"Wait," Colt said, grabbing Blue's complete attention. "What is it?"

Then Colt cursed. "I found something. *Blood.* And lots of it."

Chapter Twelve

Blood.

Considering her queasy stomach, it wasn't a good thing to keep thinking about, but Rayanne couldn't get it off her mind.

Blood that Colt had found near the car parked by Tucker's house. Fresh blood that indicated a fresh, possibly fatal wound despite the fact that so far they had found no body, and no one had shown up at E.R.s in the area sporting a wound that could have produced that amount of blood.

It'd cost her a good night's sleep, and she figured it would continue to cost her until she learned if the blood belonged to Woody or the assassin who'd tried to kill Blue and her. She was praying it was the assassin, but if it was, then why hadn't Woody contacted them?

Or maybe the blood was from both men, the result of an attack that left them both injured. They could have both managed to escape. Maybe they were in hiding and tending their wounds. She hadn't heard any gunshots, but that didn't mean the men hadn't used other weapons.

Woody could be out there somewhere, bleeding.

Dying, even.

With that unpleasant thought repeating in her head,

Rayanne gave up on another attempt to sleep, threw back the covers and got up. She caught a glimpse of herself in the chrome base of the lamp on her nightstand. Even with her reflection distorted, the lack of sleep was evident all over her face.

She checked her phone again, something she'd been doing throughout the night, hoping that by some miracle she'd somehow missed a call with an update on the investigation. An update to tell her that everything was okay. Bad guys had been caught. The danger had passed.

No missed calls, though.

The sun had just come up, the light spearing through the edges of the curtains, and outside, she heard sounds of the ranch hands, their day already beginning. Normally, she'd be starting it right along with them. Doing whatever needed to be done.

Riding fence.

Checking on the new foals.

Anything to stay busy and keep her mind off her mother's upcoming trial and her daily contact with a father and brothers who resented her being there. And she kept busy to keep her mind off Blue.

Of course, she was no longer grieving his death in between the bouts of cursing him for walking out on her.

No.

With Blue under the same roof, she was cursing him for a different reason.

He'd disappeared to save her. Then he had returned to save her. And he just kept on trying to save her. As if she needed a cowboy hero in a leather vest to do that.

Okay, it was nice to have one, especially when that protection included the baby.

However, her vest-wearing hero only added to her

worries, too. She couldn't risk that kind of hurt again, no matter how many times Blue saved her. She couldn't go back to that dark place that she'd barely managed to claw her way out of five months ago.

"Relationships," she mumbled like profanity.

Well, at least one relationship hadn't kept her up all night. Thanks to Seth's prodding, Rosalie would be leaving for a safe house soon. Of course, Seth's prodding hadn't worked on Rayanne. She had no intention of dropping the investigation and going into hiding.

Blue wouldn't, either.

And that was another reason for her to stay put. He would never admit it to her, but he was nowhere near 100 percent, and that bum shoulder could get him killed the hard way.

The sound of hurried footsteps in the hall got her jumping to her feet. Rayanne braced herself for a knock. And for more bad news. But no knock. The door flew open, and a naked Blue came rushing in.

Well, he was nearly naked, anyway.

She'd noticed the naked parts first. His bare chest. Bare feet. In fact, the only clothing he had on was his jeans, and they weren't even fully zipped.

Rayanne hated that she noticed he was commando.

Heck, she wasn't faring much better in the clothing department, and Blue noticed, too. She was wearing just a T-shirt that didn't cover much, especially since there was more of her to cover these days.

"What's wrong now?" she asked because it had to be something bad for him to come rushing in here half-dressed.

Rayanne braced herself for news that the assassin had

been spotted near, or in, the house. But that was when she realized that Blue didn't even have his gun.

Blue shook his head as if to clear it, and he tore his attention from the T-shirt that barely covered her bottom. He bolted toward her and hauled her into his arms.

"I got my memory back." His words rushed together, the excitement and breath in his voice. "When I woke up, it was just there."

"All of it?" she asked.

"I think so. Go ahead, test me on something. *Anything.*"

Sadly, the thing that came to mind first and foremost was the part about them landing in bed. Since he was half-naked and totally happy and she was in his arms, it was best to go with something much safer.

"How about the conversations you had with Woody right before you faked your death? Do your memories mesh with what Woody told us?" she asked.

He nodded, pulled back, and his grip melted off her. That question also melted some of the giddiness in his eyes. "Yeah, and that means Woody probably risked his life coming here and telling us everything he knew."

"Probably?" she questioned.

"I have no idea what's been going on with Woody for the past five months. Yes, he came here to give us that information, but we can't completely trust his motives."

Blue was right and still doing everything to protect her. Even if it meant not trusting an agent he'd once trusted with his life. After all, Woody could be trying to cover up his involvement in those guns that had made it back into the wrong hands.

"So where were you all these months?" Rayanne risked asking.

And it was a risk.

Because he might tell her a truth that she wasn't ready to hear. Just in case, Rayanne turned away so he wouldn't be able to see her face. He'd already seen her cry in the past twenty-four hours, and that was more than enough. Best not to let him see any pain that this might bring to the surface.

"After I left and faked my death, I kept you under surveillance," he said after taking a deep breath. "I had to make sure Gandy or whoever was behind the kidnapping-hit order didn't go after you."

Strange. She'd felt his presence but had dismissed it because of her sheer anger at his hasty, unexplained departure.

"I never saw you," she settled for saying.

"That must mean I'm pretty good at my job." He added that carefully, as if he sensed something was wrong. It was. This conversation was scaring the heck out of her.

"What'd you do then?" she pressed.

"I kept investigating. Kept looking for answers. Then three days ago I heard from a criminal informant that someone was hiring for a hit on you."

Even though she already knew that, it was still hard to hear. Even harder to feel it. Had the person who'd ordered the hit known she was pregnant? If so, that made him a special kind of monster.

"I didn't know that Woody had essentially blown my fake-death cover," Blue continued a moment later, "so I posed as a triggerman willing to do the hit on you. I came here to the ranch to warn you, but those men caught up with me before I could do that."

Yes, and now the burning question was, who had hired those men?

If they could just catch the remaining assassin, alive, then he might be willing to cut a plea deal, give them answers and put an end to this. Of course, if Woody or Caleb had been the one to hire him, he would be even more hesitant to speak to anyone in law enforcement.

"I know what's bothering you," Blue tossed out there like a gauntlet. "The wording might not be exact, but you said once I got my memory back, then I'd know more of how I felt about what happened between us."

Rayanne pulled in her breath and was glad she wasn't facing him.

"That night, after we made love, you said you'd take a bullet for me," Blue reminded her.

Really? Of all the things that had gone on, why had he remembered that?

"I was caught up in the moment," she insisted. Rayanne no longer had any idea if that was even the truth. "I figured that's why you left the way you did."

"What?" Blue stepped in front of her.

No more hiding her face, so Rayanne tried to hide any hurt that might be there.

"What else was I to think?" She shrugged. "Even though it was just a slip of the tongue, I'd never said anything like that to anyone but family, and then you up and disappeared. I thought you got spooked because maybe you believed I was looking for a commitment."

Blue just stared at her as if she'd sprouted an extra eyeball.

Rayanne threw her hands in the air. "Look, I don't have a lot of experience with relationships, okay? I'm not exactly a warm, open person."

"But you are."

That hung in the air for several moments before he

huffed and continued. "All of this tough-girl stuff is just a wall you put up because it crushed you when your father didn't fight for you to stay at the ranch. He sent you and your sister packing, but he kept his sons. That cut you to the core."

She hated that Blue was right.

Hated even more that he could see through her so easily.

That wall was the only thing that'd allowed her to survive, and she couldn't tear it down yet.

Not even for Blue.

"Whatever," Rayanne mumbled, and she silently cursed the tears she felt threatening. "I just want you to know that I'm taking back that bullet remark. I didn't mean it."

His hands went on his hips. "You're sure?"

"Of course."

Either she hadn't said it with enough conviction or else he flat-out didn't believe her.

"Good," he said. "I don't want you taking any bullets for me."

All right. That went along with the hero stuff and watching over that he'd been doing. But she figured he knew that taking a bullet was just another version of the *L* word. And it was a word that didn't apply here.

She hoped.

Blue wasn't a man to play around with. Beneath those hot cowboy looks was a dark agent who likely had as much fear of the word as she did.

"Are you wearing panties under that T-shirt?" he asked.

Of all the things she'd expected him to say next, that wasn't one of them. Though she had noticed that his gaze kept drifting in that direction. Just as hers kept going to that open flap in his jeans.

"Yes," she snapped. Barely there panties but still panties nonetheless.

He made a slight sound of disappointment, went to the door, shut it and then came back her way.

"I'm going to tell you something," Blue said. "And then I'm going to kiss you."

Again, he'd managed to surprise her. And fire up some heat inside her. This conversation was certainly going in a strange direction.

Rayanne dropped back a step, and her gaze automatically went to his bare chest and unzipped jeans. There was a thin line of dark hair that arrowed down from his navel right to the part that his zipper barely covered.

That part of him and the threat of a kiss had her going all warm and golden.

Exactly what she didn't need.

"You think kissing me is a smart thing to do?" she asked, and kept her gaze on that zipper so he'd know exactly what she meant. Talk about playing with fire.

"No, I think it'll be a really stupid thing to do, but I'm doing it, anyway. And I promise it won't go any further than kissing. After…"

But he stopped, shook his head, and then without even getting into the *telling her something,* Blue pulled her to him and kissed her.

Oh, mercy.

She'd never gotten a bad kiss from Blue, but this one immediately hit all the right buttons. The firm pressure of his mouth on hers.

His taste. His scent.

The way he hooked his arm around her and drew her close. Closer.

Until she was plastered right against him.

All the memories came flooding back to her, too. The ones she'd tried to push aside of just how good, and hot, Blue could make her feel.

Even when it wasn't a good idea for her to be feeling these things.

There was the whole issue of him being nearly naked. Her blasted hormone issues, too. Plus the investigation they should be doing.

But did any of those things stop her?

Nope.

Rayanne just stood there and took everything he was giving her, and it didn't take her body long to start wrestling to bring him even closer, to deepen the kiss even more.

To make sure this mistake was one worth making.

She felt herself moving and realized that Blue was maneuvering them toward the wall. Her back landed against the smooth, cool surface, and even though he stayed gentle, the hunger she could feel inside herself was the exact opposite of gentle.

Rayanne ached for him.

Ached to have him take her the way he had that night five months ago.

And Blue didn't disappoint.

"Just kisses," he repeated.

He moved those kisses to her neck. Right to the spot that he knew would make her melt. And it did. Rayanne couldn't stop the sound of pleasure that escaped from her mouth.

That sound must have been like an invitation to Blue.

That and the fact that she wasn't doing a darn thing to stop this. She certainly didn't stop him when Blue caught on to the bottom of her T-shirt and shoved it up.

"You weren't lying about the panties," he mumbled, his mouth now against her breasts. He slid his hands into the back of the panties, to her bottom, inching down the panties in the same motion.

"You said just kisses," she reminded him.

"Yeah, but I didn't limit them to your mouth."

With that, he dropped to his knees and gave her a kiss that had Rayanne making more than just a little sound. She had to clamp her teeth over her bottom lip to stop herself from letting the rest of the house know what was going on.

Blue slid her knee on his shoulder—thankfully, the one without the bandage—and he just kept on *kissing.*

Rayanne gave up any thoughts of stopping this and instead anchored herself by sliding one hand against the wall. The other she sank deep into his hair.

It didn't take much before she felt her body clench. Before the ripples started and turned to a full-blown earthquake. The pleasure swooshed through every inch of her, and she would have fallen if Blue hadn't been right there to catch her.

Rayanne was still trying to gather her breath and come back to earth when Blue took hold of her and eased her to a sitting position on the bed.

"No," he said, following the direction of her gaze to the hard bulge behind the partly open zipper of his jeans. "You're not going to do anything about that."

"Why not?" she blurted out. It wasn't a good question, especially since she knew the answer. This wasn't the time for "one good turn deserves another."

"Because it won't stay just a kiss. I'll have you on that bed, and those little lace panties won't be much of a barrier to stopping us."

She was having a hard time remembering why that wouldn't be a good idea. Oh, yes. Because it would be a major distraction. And maybe make his injuries even worse. Blue wasn't in any shape for sex, even if her body was trying to convince her otherwise.

Rayanne shook her head. "Are you in pain?" And now her gaze shifted to his shoulder.

The corner of his mouth lifted. "Not that kind of pain." He finally did something about that flapping zipper. He closed it, not easily, but after some wincing, he got himself fully covered.

Peep show over.

Something she shouldn't have been so disappointed about. But she was.

"Why'd you do that?" she asked.

"I couldn't stop myself. I should apologize, I know, but an *I'm sorry* would be a lie. I'm not sorry, and we didn't get a chance to do that the night we were together."

No, that night had happened in a heated rush. The culmination of weeks of hot smoldering looks and lust-filled thoughts. Well, on her part, anyway. Judging from what'd just gone on between them, it'd been the same for Blue.

"You didn't tell me what you wanted to say," she reminded him. Best to move this conversation from well-placed kisses to something safer.

He stared at her, and his jaw muscles stirred. "It's personal…."

"You're married," she blurted out.

He laughed. It was smoky and thick and brought back some wonderful memories. "No. Not married."

Blue didn't get a chance to tell her what he'd wanted to say, because his phone rang. Rayanne groaned not just because of the interruption but because a call this time of morning couldn't be good news.

"It's Caleb," he said after fishing his phone from his jeans pocket.

Definitely not good news. Except that maybe Blue and she would finally learn what the heck was going on with Caleb.

"Where are you?" Blue demanded the moment he answered and put the call on speaker.

"Look outside. We need to talk."

Chapter Thirteen

"Don't go near that window," Blue warned Rayanne.

He put Caleb on hold and hurried back across the hall to grab the rest of his clothes.

And his gun.

A weapon wasn't something he'd ever thought he would need just to talk to his former boss, but Blue wasn't taking any chances. Especially since he'd already taken a huge one just with the morning *kissing* session with Rayanne.

Talk about the fastest way to lose focus, and this call from Caleb was a gigantic reminder that what Blue should be focusing on was unraveling this dangerous puzzle that could get Rayanne and the baby hurt.

While he kept Caleb on hold, Blue dressed and went to the window. Rayanne did, too, and she took her gun from the nightstand, but she stayed behind him when Blue eased back the curtains and opened the blinds.

Yeah, Caleb was there, all right.

He was standing on the road that led to the house and was surrounded by three armed ranch hands, exactly as they'd been for Wendell's and Woody's visits.

Caleb had his phone sandwiched between his ear and shoulder, and both hands were in the air. A black four-door sedan was parked about twenty yards behind him, and the passenger's-side door was open. He'd likely parked there and walked.

But why?

Maybe because the hands hadn't given him a choice, but if so, then had the hands allowed the man closer to the house? Blue made a mental note to instruct them not to do that again. Caleb, or any of their other suspects, could be dangerous.

"Tell the men to back down," Caleb insisted when Blue took the call off hold.

"Not until I get some answers, and they'd better be good answers, too. I know what's going on with you. By the way, Hale said to give you a message—either come in or give up your badge."

Caleb cursed, and even from a distance, Blue could see the frustration on the man's face. He could also see that Caleb was disheveled, his clothes wrinkled. Definitely not the polished agent who'd visited him in the hospital just two days earlier to move him to a "safer" location.

Or maybe move him so he could kill him.

"I was set up," Caleb immediately volunteered.

That would explain why his former boss was suddenly on the wrong side of the law.

Well, it would explain it if he was telling the truth. Of course, Blue knew a thing or two about being set up since someone had tried to do the same to him with that hit order on Rayanne.

"Tell me about those weapons that I confiscated earlier this year," Blue said to Caleb. "The ones that got back into the wrong hands."

"I will, but I'd rather not talk about that while standing out here in the open at gunpoint. I'm not armed. My gun's on the ground."

It was. Blue could see it next to one of the hands. But that didn't mean Caleb didn't have a backup weapon on him somewhere, and even if one of the hands had frisked him, Caleb knew how to hide a gun.

"We'll stick with this arrangement for now," Blue informed him. "I want to know about those guns and why Hale thinks you might be dirty."

Caleb looked up at the house, and his gaze rifled across the windows until he spotted Blue. The muscles in his face tightened. Blue knew pure anger when he saw it. But why the heck was that anger directed at him?

"Hale thinks I'm dirty," Caleb finally answered, "because like I said, somebody set me up."

Blue's next questions were simple. Maybe Caleb would have simple, believable answers. "Who and how?"

Caleb shook his head and gave a weary sigh. "I don't know who did it, but they used a hacker to get into the Justice Department files and plant info about me." He paused. "I thought it might be you."

Well, that explained the angry face. "Me? Why the hell would I do that?"

"To stop me from arresting you," Caleb snapped.

"You've got no cause to arrest me. And besides, I haven't exactly had time to set anyone up. Someone's been trying to kill me, remember?"

"Yes." That was all Caleb said for several moments. "I remember. Do you?"

Blue debated what exactly to tell him and decided to go with the truth to see how Caleb would react. "I remember *everything*."

For just a moment he thought he saw a flash of concern in Caleb's eyes, and Blue wished he was closer so he could figure out what it meant.

"Good," Caleb answered, after that unexplained flash. "Then you know I'm not dirty."

"Sorry, the only thing I know is someone's trying to kidnap or kill Rayanne and me, and you're on a short list of suspects."

Now he got more than a flash of a reaction. Caleb cursed. "That's why I wanted this meeting. I put my neck on the line, maybe literally, and I did that so both of us could get answers. Rayanne, too. It's not a good idea for the baby and her to keep dodging bullets."

Rayanne groaned softly. Neither of them had told him about the pregnancy. Of course, now that Rayanne was showing, he could have noticed it or even heard it around town. Still, coming from Caleb, it sounded a little like a threat.

"Do you agree we need to end the danger and clear our names?" Caleb asked.

"My name's cleared." Blue hoped. "And how do you plan to end the danger?"

"For starters, this meeting. I didn't come alone." Caleb tipped his head to his car. "I thought it was time we all sat down and talked."

Oh, Blue didn't like the sound of that. And he really didn't like it when the back doors of Caleb's car opened.

And two men stepped out.

JUDGING FROM BLUE'S mumbled profanity, Rayanne figured she wasn't going to be pleased with whomever Caleb had brought with him.

And she wasn't.

When Rayanne looked over Blue's shoulder, she spotted the unholy pair.

Wendell Braddock and Rex Gandy.

Coupled with Caleb, they represented all their suspects, gathered practically right at the doorstep. She hadn't wanted them in the same state with Blue, her and her family, much less this close. The only one missing was Woody, and with the way their luck had been running, he might just get out of that car, too, and confess that all four of them were working to kill Blue and her.

"Stay to the side of the window," Blue told her.

She did, but Rayanne positioned herself so she could still see the men. She wanted to watch their expressions in case they showed any signs of guilt. Of course, in Gandy's case, he was probably a sociopath and therefore too good at hiding what was really going on in his head.

"You shouldn't have brought them here," Blue said, his voice a low, dangerous warning and his attention nailed to Caleb.

"Trust me, I didn't want to do that," Caleb answered, adding yet another surprise to this meeting. He took his phone from his ear and pressed a button, no doubt to put it on speaker so the other men could hear the conversation. "They didn't give me much of a choice."

"I don't see you being held at gunpoint," Rayanne remarked. "That means you had a choice. Plus, Wendell accused you of being a dirty agent, so I have no idea why you'd let him get in your car."

"Wendell's accused people of a lot of things," Gandy volunteered, earning a glare from Wendell.

Strange bedfellows indeed.

"I was on my way out here," Caleb said, "and these two were stopped at the end of the road."

"And when the agent here said he was coming out to visit y'all," Gandy continued, "we decided to all come together and speak our piece at once."

"*You* decided," Caleb corrected. "And you threatened to call my boss and tell him where I was if I didn't cooperate. That's the only reason I let you in the car."

Interesting. Or maybe just a flat-out lie. Rayanne really hoped they weren't all in this together. If they were, then at best it was a tenuous partnership since there wasn't a shred of trust among them.

"You weren't afraid one of these stellar citizens would kill you?" Rayanne asked Caleb.

Caleb eyed them both like a pair of rattlesnakes. "Like I said, I didn't have much of a choice. I came because I need to do something, anything, to save my badge."

Rayanne didn't intend to feel any sympathy for him, at least not until Caleb was totally cleared as a suspect. She seriously doubted that would happen with this meeting.

"And Blue didn't give us a choice, either," Wendell insisted. "You're fueling an investigation and dragging us all into it."

"Because one of you likely hired that trio of killers who came to the ranch," Blue fired back.

Gandy rolled his eyes. "Always trying to get in your jabs, aren't you? And where have those jabs got you so far? Nowhere. You've never uncovered a single piece of evidence that could lead to my arrest."

"The day's not over," Blue mumbled.

Gandy chuckled. "Never liked your methods, Blue, but I gotta say, I always admired your persistence. Except in this case, persistence is causing a whole bunch of cops and such to pester me with questions. I want it stopped."

"Yeah," Wendell agreed. "And that's why we need to

sit down and talk. Caleb here wants to save his badge, but I've got a reputation to salvage. I do business with a lot of important people who wouldn't be happy to learn I'm the subject of an investigation, even if it's a witch hunt."

"It's not a witch hunt. And you're not getting in this house," Blue informed them. "Talking won't help...unless one of you plans to make a full confession."

"Nothing to confess to," Gandy said, and the other two mumbled some form of agreement. "Now, the person you should be looking at is your old pal Woody Janson. I've heard rumblings of some confiscated guns making it back into criminals' hands. Who better to do that than Woody?"

Blue and she just stared at Caleb.

"Blue thinks I'm responsible for that," Caleb volunteered. "And since I haven't had the opportunity to talk to Woody, I can't question him about it. But my money's on him, too."

"Yeah, especially since Woody survived the attack and all," Gandy tossed out there.

That got her attention.

Rayanne moved so she could get a better look at the man. Gandy was gloating, probably because he knew he'd just dropped a bombshell.

Even Caleb and Wendell seemed surprised by Gandy's comment. But it could be fake. She still wasn't sure they were here only to convince Blue to back off an investigation that could save their lives.

"How'd you know that Woody survived?" Rayanne asked.

Gandy lifted his shoulder as if the answer were obvious. "Word gets around fast when a former employee of questionable integrity turns up dead."

Blue and she exchanged a glance. "What would that have to do with Woody?" Blue asked, obviously not volunteering anything about Woody's visit.

"Plenty and you know it," Gandy fired back.

"Why don't you fill me in on the plenty that I know," Blue said, his voice dripping with sarcasm.

Gandy smiled as if he was getting a lot of pleasure from this. "A friend of a friend told me that a guy named Ace Butler turned up in a hospital down in Floresville. Ace had been shot, didn't make it through surgery, but his lawyer showed up and tried to pay the doc to stay quiet about it."

"His lawyer?" Blue questioned.

Gandy shrugged. "Or maybe it was just an acquaintance, but the point is—check out Ace and see if he's the clown who tried to kill you two days ago. And if he was, then I'm figuring he had a little run-in with Woody yesterday."

Blue and she had already seen the photo of the man by Woody's car and knew that he was the same idiot who'd come to the ranch to kill them. There'd also been the blood found near Woody's car, and it was still at the lab for DNA testing. If it proved to be a match to this Ace Butler, then it meant Gandy was telling the truth.

Or at least a partial truth.

But why?

Gandy wasn't the sort to volunteer anything unless it benefited him, and in this case, he was probably hoping that the info would put the blame for the attacks on someone other than himself.

"I'll call Seth," Rayanne whispered to Blue.

While Blue stayed at the window, she stepped to the other side of the room to make the call. She filled her brother in on what Gandy had just told them so he could check out the hospital in Floresville.

"How exactly did you come by all this information?" Blue asked Gandy when Rayanne finished her call.

"I'd rather not say," Gandy answered.

"I'd rather you did," Blue snapped.

Gandy's mouth stretched as if he was about to smile or stall them again.

But he didn't get a chance to do or say anything.

Caleb pivoted, his attention rifling behind them. "Get down!" he shouted.

Just as a shot rang out.

Chapter Fourteen

Blue cursed.

From the moment he'd seen Caleb outside the ranch house, he'd figured that trouble wouldn't be far behind. Too bad he'd been right.

He didn't have to tell Rayanne to get down. She ducked to the side of the window, her gun ready in her hand.

Blue positioned himself on the other side, and he put his phone on the windowsill to free up his hands in case he had to return fire or protect Rayanne.

It might come down to both.

"Who fired the shot?" Rayanne asked.

But Blue had to shake his head. From what he could see, it certainly wasn't any of their "guests" or the three armed ranch hands guarding them. All six men went to the ground, scrambling to take cover in front of and around Caleb's car. Caleb snatched up his gun from the ground, and both Wendell and Gandy drew theirs.

Right before the sound of another shot blasted through the air.

The bullet slammed into the ground right in the spot where one of the ranch hands had just been standing, and again, it hadn't come from any of the six.

It'd come from behind them.

From the woods.

"Who's shooting out there?" Blue heard Roy call out. He didn't sound close but rather on the first floor near the stairs.

"We're not sure yet. Who else is in the house?" Blue asked the man.

"Right now it's just me and the housekeeper, Mary. Colt's already left for work. Rosalie's still at the guest cottage. She was supposed to be leaving for the safe house in an hour or so."

Well, that wouldn't happen until this situation was under control.

"Call Rosalie now. Tell her to take cover," Rayanne insisted. "And Mary and you need to do the same," she added, but it wasn't with the same desperate urgency that she'd given to her twin sister.

Blue heard the fear in Rayanne's voice. Saw it more in her face and body language, and he cursed. She and the baby were right back in danger again, and so far he hadn't been able to do a darn thing to stop these attacks from happening. Now here they were right smack-dab in the middle of another one.

"You should call your brothers Tucker and Cooper," Blue reminded Rayanne. "They might not have left for work yet."

Even though they didn't live in the main house, they both had places nearby and both had children. Of course, if they were home, they'd likely already heard the shots and had taken cover, but Blue wanted to make sure.

She nodded, started making the calls, which seemed to help steady her nerves. Good. Anything to keep her stress level down and get her mind focused on something other than the bullets flying.

"Tucker and his family are still out of town," she relayed. "Cooper's at his place. He's staying put to watch his wife and son, but he's called for backup."

Good. Blue was afraid they might need it. There were a lot of possible targets at the ranch, and he didn't want anyone getting hurt. Or anyone being used to draw out Rayanne and him.

"What the hell's going on?" Caleb asked. "Is it one of the hired hands shooting at us?"

"No." Blue hoped not, anyway. "The shots are probably coming from the woods across the road."

A second later Blue was able to eliminate the *probably* when the next shot rang out.

Yeah, it'd definitely come from the woods.

Blue could pinpoint the general area of the shooter, but he still didn't see anyone. Of course, the guy could be perched behind or even up in some of the live-oak trees, which were still green and thick with leaves.

Another shot.

This one slammed into Caleb's car, pinging off the back bumper, and it was close enough to send the men scrambling again. Gandy reached up, opened the back door and dived inside. Wendell crawled beneath the car and out of sight. The ranch hands hurried to the sides of the porch.

Caleb threw open the driver's-side door, too, but he didn't get in. He used the door for cover and took aim at whoever was shooting at them from the woods. He didn't fire, probably because he knew the shooter was out of range of his Glock. Of course, he might have held fire for another reason.

Because he could be responsible for this entire mess.

Heck, any of the three men out there could be.

Maybe the culprit thought it would take suspicion off himself if he was in the center of an attack like this, but if so, Blue wasn't buying it. So far none of the shots had gone anywhere near their suspects, and that meant any one of them could have orchestrated this.

"Are you just gonna let this go on?" Wendell shouted. Even though the man was no longer near Caleb's phone, Blue heard him loud and clear.

Blue didn't get a chance to answer Wendell, because the next two bullets slammed through the window right next to Blue's head. Glass spewed over the room, and Blue practically threw himself over Rayanne to stop her from being cut or worse.

The pain shot through him, and it took Blue a moment to realize he hadn't been shot again. He'd just knocked his shoulder against the wall. He tried to muffle any sound of pain. Failed. And that brought Rayanne off the floor.

There was fire in her eyes, and she tried to bolt to the window, no doubt so she could try to shoot back.

Blue didn't let that happen.

No way would he allow her to put herself in harm's way, so Blue held on to her and wrestled her back to the floor. That didn't help the pain, but because of the hold he had on her, she wasn't in the line of fire when the next bullet came crashing into the room.

The shot slammed into the floor.

Outside, there were other shots. So many that Blue wondered if there was more than one shooter. Heck, maybe the moron behind this had sent an entire army after them.

"I'm hit!" Blue heard Caleb shout through the gaping holes in the window.

Blue scrambled closer, took a quick look outside and

saw Caleb. His former boss was still behind his car door. He had his gun in his right hand, which was also clamped around his left forearm.

And, yeah, there was blood.

"I'm calling Cooper to make sure he's sending an ambulance," Rayanne mumbled. Though both knew the medics wouldn't come into the middle of a shoot-out.

"I'm coming in," Roy warned them, and several seconds later the door flew open.

"Stay down!" Blue ordered, but Rayanne's father was already doing that.

Roy was practically on the floor, a rifle with a scope in one hand and binoculars in the other, and he crawled his way to them.

"Are you all right?" Roy asked, giving both of them glances.

"We weren't hit," Blue settled for saying, but he still had to take some deep breaths to force back the pain. Mercy, this was not a good time for his injury to rear its ugly head.

"How's Rosalie?" Rayanne asked her father.

"She's okay. I told her to go into the bathroom at the guesthouse and get in the shower. It's got a stone surface, and it's the safest place to be in case a bullet ricochets in her direction."

It was, and with the bullets flying, hopefully Rosalie would stay put until this was over. While he was hoping, Blue added that maybe this attack was just limited to the idiot firing at them.

"Maybe I can help," Roy said. "No need for Rayanne to be in the middle of this." His gaze dropped to her stomach. He didn't mention the baby. Didn't have to.

"I'm fine, *really,*" Rayanne snapped, but she didn't

stop Roy from taking up position at the side of the window where she'd just been.

Roy nodded, and if his daughter's curt assurance hurt his feelings, he sure didn't show it. Probably because he was focused on stopping the danger to her and his unborn grandchild.

"There's an old tree house in one of the live oaks out in those woods," Roy said, peering through the binoculars. "The boys built it there years ago, but if it's still sturdy enough, I'm betting that's where the shooter is."

Roy passed the binoculars to Blue. "Look at the tallest tree and see if you can make out anything."

Blue gave it a try, but he saw only the leaves, not a shooter. However, he did see remnants of a tree house. There was enough of it left that it would have made an excellent hiding place for a sniper attack.

"Since your shoulder's messed up, maybe you'd like for me to try to take him out," Roy offered. "This rifle's got a kick, and it won't feel so good when it hits those stitches."

The man was right about that, but Blue wasn't exactly eager to put Roy right in the middle of this fight. Except he already was since the shooter was firing into the house. Still firing outside, too. Several bullets smacked into Caleb's car and the ground around it.

Roy maneuvered closer to the window but had to quickly duck when another bullet slammed into the room. Obviously, this idiot had them in his sights, but maybe Blue could do something to distract him.

"Grab that chrome lamp," Blue told Rayanne, tipping his head to the nightstand. "Don't come any closer but slide it across the floor toward me."

It took her a moment to get it unplugged, and she used

her foot to get it to him. There was plenty of sunlight now, and he hoped the glare off the chrome would shield Roy from the shooter so Rayanne's father could get off a shot.

Blue looked at Roy, and when the man gave him a nod, Blue moved the lamp onto the windowsill. In the same motion, Roy took aim with the rifle.

And he fired.

The blast was heavy and thick, echoing through Blue's head, and Roy quickly followed it up with another shot. He'd been right about that kick. Both times the impact jerked back Roy's shoulder.

Blue looked through the binoculars and finally spotted something.

Or rather *someone*.

He caught just a glimpse of a man dressed in dark clothes scrambling down from what was left of that tree house.

"Shoot at him again," Blue told Roy.

Roy quickly took aim and sent two more bullets the guy's way. Blue couldn't tell if he hit him or not, but the gunman stopped firing.

It suddenly got so quiet that the only sound came from their heavy breathing and the cool morning air rushing through what was left of the window.

Then the sirens in the distance.

Backup. Maybe an ambulance, too.

Blue had another look with the binoculars, moving the sights from the tree house to the ground below it.

Oh, mercy.

There was the shooter, all right, and he was running. Getting away. And there was nothing Blue could do about it.

His lawman's instinct was to hurry out of the room

and go after him. To catch him and force him to tell them what was going on.

But doing that would mean leaving Rayanne in the house.

Yeah, her father was there, but if there was indeed an army out there ready to attack, Blue wanted to be close to her and not out in the woods chasing down a triggerman. In fact, this could be yet another ruse to draw him out so that Rayanne would be an easier target.

"He got away?" Rayanne asked, obviously picking up on Blue's body language.

He nodded.

She mumbled some profanity and made a call to tell Cooper that it was safe enough for backup and the ambulance to come closer.

It didn't take long for the sirens to get louder, and Blue glanced down at the yard to check on everyone's locations. And to make sure none of the suspects were about to turn a gun in Blue's direction.

But Blue didn't like what he saw.

Or rather what he didn't see.

Caleb was no longer by the car door, and with the bullets flying, Blue had lost sight of him. There was no sign of Gandy or Wendell, either. Maybe they were still in hiding, but Blue didn't like the knot that tightened in his gut.

Something was wrong.

"Wait here with your dad," Blue told Rayanne.

She was shaking her head before he even got to his feet. "The shooter could come back, or he could still be waiting out there for you."

"I figure he's long gone." And likely regrouping for another attack. That was something Blue kept to himself, though Rayanne probably already knew. "Just please stay put."

Whether she would or not was anyone's guess, but he brushed a kiss on her forehead, hoping it would remind her that he had her best interest at heart. For good measure, he dropped a kiss on her stomach, too.

"You're playing dirty," she grumbled.

"Yeah," he readily admitted. And he kissed her on the mouth, too.

That probably earned him a glare, but Blue didn't take the time to verify it. With his gun still ready and gripped in his hand, he went down the stairs and peered out the sidelight windows.

He still couldn't see anything.

Where the heck were they?

However, when he eased open the front door, he spotted the ranch hands still on the sides of the house, and Cooper was making his way on foot toward them. Cooper's own house was just yards away, and another of the hands, Arlene, was standing guard on his front porch. Probably because Cooper's family was still inside.

"Is everyone okay?" Cooper called out to him.

Blue nodded. "Your dad's upstairs with Rayanne."

Cooper lifted his eyebrow. He didn't say anything, but the surprise was in his eyes, verifying what Blue had already guessed. That Rayanne and her father didn't interact much.

Well, until this morning.

Roy had likely saved their lives. That would create an interaction whether Rayanne liked it or not.

"You look like crap," Cooper said to him. "Are you in pain?"

"Some," Blue admitted. "Not enough to stop me from helping you catch this jerk."

"I'd rather you help by staying put. I don't want anyone getting upstairs to Dad. Or Rayanne," Cooper added, and he shot a glance at the car.

Where he'd last seen their three suspects.

Blue doubted any of them would bolt toward the house, but it wasn't a risk he was willing to take. Rayanne and the baby had already been through enough today, and one of the men could be a killer.

The sirens stopped when an ambulance pulled into the drive. Colt was right behind them in a cruiser. The medics stayed put, but Colt got out, and along with Cooper, they started to converge on Caleb's car.

"Is everyone all right?" Cooper shouted.

If anyone answered, Blue wasn't able to hear them. He could only watch as Cooper and Colt made it to the car. Their guns drawn. Their attention nailed to the interior of the vehicle, probably in case one of their suspects came out shooting.

Colt went to the left side of the car, Cooper the right. Both pivoted, aiming their guns.

And Cooper cursed. He looked up, his gaze meeting Blue's. "He's been shot."

"Who? Caleb?" Blue asked.

Cooper shook his head. "Rex Gandy. And from the looks of it, he's dead."

Chapter Fifteen

Rayanne was afraid if she stood up from the kitchen table, her legs would give way and she'd fall. Hardly what she wanted, considering she felt wimpy enough without doing something to prove it.

This pregnancy had changed everything.

And Blue had, too.

Six months ago she would have taken on that shooter and not batted an eye. Well, she was doing more than eye batting now. It sickened her to think of how close Blue, she and the baby had come to dying again. It sickened her even more to know that the threat likely hadn't been stopped.

Not even with Gandy's death.

Because they still didn't know how the man had died. Or why. Until they learned that, the threat was still just as real and fresh as it had been two days ago when her life had turned on a dime.

"You need to eat," Blue prompted her, pulling his attention from his latest phone call so he could slide the sandwich and glass of milk closer to her.

Rayanne picked up the sandwich, only because Blue, Rosalie and Roy were all giving her concerned looks.

Heck, even Colt seemed worried about her. A first.

Well, a first since she'd returned to the ranch. Once, a million years ago, Colt and she had been close.

They were all in the massive kitchen at the ranch. All of them, except her, contributing in some way to the investigation and crime-scene cleanup. Rosalie had checked Blue's bandage several times and was now helping Mary make sandwiches for everyone. Colt and Blue were making nonstop calls. Roy was going over instructions with Arlene on how to beef up security.

Cooper was no doubt making calls back at his own place, where he could better watch his wife and son. Rayanne couldn't blame him. The latest attack had literally been too close to home, and like Roy, he would need to make his own security arrangements.

"I'm okay," Rayanne insisted when Blue continued to stare at her.

She took a large exaggerated bite from the ham-and-cheese sandwich. It tasted like dust. Probably because her mouth was bone-dry and the last thing her stomach wanted her to do was put food in it. Her mind was numb from the adrenaline that'd come and gone, leaving her exhausted.

Blue finished his call with the Floresville P.D., scrubbed his hand over his face and looked at her again. "After you eat, you should get some rest."

She would have bet the balance of her checking account that he was going to say that. "Ditto. I'm not the one healing from a gunshot wound and a concussion. Now, what did you learn about Ace Butler? Did he really die in the Floresville hospital or not?"

"He died, all right. His prints were in the system, and they're a match to the body. There's no surveillance footage of the person who tried to bribe the doctor to keep it quiet, but the cops are interviewing people who might have seen him."

Rayanne had to fight through the fatigue to process that. "So Gandy was telling the truth."

Interesting. Gandy was dead, so he couldn't tell them why he'd doled out that info to them. Or why he'd given them the photo and audio clip. Rayanne had figured it was so it would make him seem innocent, and in light of his death, maybe he *was* innocent.

About this, anyway.

Now the question was, had Gandy's death been by accident or by design? It might be a while before the CSIs could give them an answer to that since Rayanne wasn't even sure they'd be able to recover the bullet from Gandy's head. Maybe fired by the sniper who'd been in the woods.

Or maybe fired by someone much closer to him.

Wendell, Caleb or even Woody.

"Caleb claims he's fine," Blue went on. Obviously, he'd learned that from his call to the Sweetwater Springs hospital, the one he had made immediately before phoning Floresville.

"'Claims he's fine,'" she repeated, studying Blue's expression while she finished off her glass of milk. "Is that ATF code for something?"

"Maybe." Blue shook his head. "Caleb's only slightly injured. In fact, the doc said it was superficial."

Sweet heaven. "So it could have been self-inflicted," Rayanne concluded. "If so, Caleb could have done that to throw suspicion off himself for the attack. He could have not only set up the attack, he could also have been the one to kill Gandy."

Blue lifted his shoulder, winced a little. That brought

Rayanne to her feet, and thankfully, she didn't wobble too much. Well, it was still enough for Blue to catch on to her arm to steady her, but she caught on to him, too.

"We're a pair," she mumbled.

"A pair who should be getting some rest," Rosalie added. "I'm not speaking as a sister now but as a nurse. Both of you are recovering from a trauma, and staying on your feet will only prolong that."

Rayanne couldn't deny that Blue could do with some rest, but she also knew how mule-headed he'd be about this. So she turned the tables on him and played the baby card. She ran her hand over her belly and gave her sister a nod.

Blue noticed the belly rub right away, and it caused a new level of alarm on his face. That got him moving, and with his arm hooked around her waist, they headed for the stairs.

"I know the drill," Rayanne said on the way up to her room. "You'll tuck me in, try to soothe my nerves and then make an excuse to come back down and work. But just know that I'm not coming up the stairs for me or the baby. We're fine. I'm doing this for you, and that means you're getting some rest."

His eyebrow slid up. "Together?"

Her eyebrow slid up, too, and she remembered the scalding-hot kissing session they'd had that morning. "Together we won't get any rest," she reminded him.

Blue chuckled, brushed a kiss on her forehead and maneuvered her into her room. "We won't if we're apart. I know the drill. You'll stew about this and wrongfully blame yourself for the danger."

"It won't be wrongful," Rayanne mumbled. "I should have figured out a way to stop the attacks. Heck, I should just leave, and at least that way, Rosalie might not be in danger—"

Blue huffed. That was the only warning before he slid his hand around the back of her neck, dragged her closer and kissed her. All in all, it was a darn effective way to shut her up, but it didn't stop the truth from being the truth.

Nor did it stop the heat from trickling through her body.

A simple kiss from Blue could do that, but it was because there was no such thing as a simple kiss from Blue. His mouth and every other part of him could cause her to melt with just a single touch. No other man had ever had that effect on her, and she prayed no other ever would.

"You have a bad habit of kissing me at the worst possible time," she mumbled against his mouth.

He eased back and met her eye to eye. "Yeah, it is a bad time." Blue glanced at the bed. Not in a let's-land-there-now kind of way. But he was no doubt thinking about how to make sure she got that rest.

She was thinking about that. And a lot of other things. Every one of those other things included Blue.

Rayanne shook her head. Opened her mouth. And she realized that what she said—or didn't say—in the next couple of seconds could change everything.

It could bring Blue closer to her.

Or keep him at bay.

The question was, what did she want to do?

She had a quick debate with her body. It didn't give her much of an argument, though. *Figures.* Neither did her heart.

And that created a huge problem for her.

After all the pain, was she willing to take that kind of a risk again?

She was still thinking about that when Blue's mouth came back to hers for another of those white-hot kisses. Then she quit thinking and debating altogether. She did something that she rarely did.

She went with her heart.

Rayanne pulled him to her and kissed him right back.

BLUE KNEW EXACTLY what Rayanne's kiss meant.

And it didn't include something she truly needed— rest.

But he was already well past the logic point here, and besides, this wasn't going to stop no matter what he said or did. There were a lot of things between Rayanne and him, and they weren't based on logic.

Blue could feel her raw need in that kiss. In the way her hand clutched him, pulling him closer and closer. Until they were plastered against each other. Since he knew this would lead them straight to the bed, he reached behind him and locked the door. If he was going to do this, then he didn't want anyone walking in on them.

"Your shoulder," Rayanne reminded him when he took those kisses to her neck.

Yeah, he was probably hurting, but his mind was shutting that out at the possibility of having Rayanne beneath him in that bed. But then he thought of another obstacle that could put this burning heat on pause.

"The pregnancy?" he said.

She huffed, pulled him right back to her. "Pregnant women can and do have sex."

Good. Because that was about the only red light that would have stopped this. That and Rayanne saying no, and it was clear from the way her grip moved from his waist to his butt that she didn't have any plans to say no.

She went after his shirt, fumbling with the buttons until she finally got it open, and her mouth landed against his chest.

Instant heat.

Not that he needed more, but Blue did take a moment to savor the feel of her lips and tongue on his bare skin. Unfortunately, that savoring turned up the urgency a significant notch, and he started to fumble with her clothes. Getting her naked became his top priority.

Her shirt was easy. He pulled it over her head and sent it sailing to the floor. Her bra quickly followed, and Blue got to return the favor of sampling Rayanne's breasts. They were full, perfect and, judging from the needy moan she made, very sensitive.

She plowed her fingers into his hair, pulling his mouth even closer so he could kiss her the way that he wanted. He went lower. To her stomach. But Rayanne pulled him back up toward her mouth.

"If those kisses go lower, we know what'll happen," she said. "This time, I want you with me."

Heck, no way could he turn down that offer. He was hard as granite, and he needed her in the worst kind of way.

She left his shirt and vest on but tackled his zipper next. No kisses. Rayanne just stared at him as the zipper went down, and Blue was able to see the fiery need in her cool gray eyes. He was sure his eyes weren't so cool when she slid her hand inside his boxers and touched him.

Oh, man.

The grunt he made sounded like pain. It wasn't.

Well, not regular pain, anyway.

This was pure pleasure.

And thankfully, Rayanne could tell the difference, because she kept touching him until Blue had no choice but to do something about the powder keg of heat that her touching had created.

Blue unzipped her jeans, which were already low on her hips to make room for her pregnant belly. He shimmied them off her, her lacy panties, too, kissing her along the way, until Rayanne obviously met her own heat threshold.

"Let's do this now," she insisted, the urgency clear in her voice.

He turned, easing her onto the bed while Rayanne continued to work on his jeans. He helped by taking off his boots and shoulder holster, and in the back of his mind, Blue was already working out the logistics of this. He didn't want to crush her and the baby with his weight, and judging from the way she was eyeing the bandage on his shoulder, she didn't want to hurt him.

Blue settled it by pulling her onto his lap. His back landed against the headboard, and Rayanne landed against him.

In all the right places.

With everything aligned just right.

Even though he had all his memories of the other time they were together, Blue still felt the jolt of surprise when he sank into her. She felt even better than he'd remembered, and what he'd remembered had been pretty darn good.

This was perfect. And mind-blowing.

Blue caught on to her hips to get her moving. Not that he had to prompt her much. Rayanne met him, pushing against him harder and faster as he pushed into her.

Still no kisses.

Just that intense eye contact that made this seem even more intimate than it already was.

"I can't last long," she said, like an apology.

But no apology was needed. This couldn't last long. The heat and the intensity just kept driving them.

Harder, faster, deeper.

Rayanne leaned in, positioning her hips, until he felt her body give way. Until he felt her slide right over the edge.

She made a sound, a silky moan of pleasure, but he saw the other emotion in her eyes. The wish that this didn't have to end so soon. Blue had the same wish, but he could only hope this wouldn't be the last time he had her like this.

Now she kissed him. Her mouth closing in over his. And that was all Blue needed to let himself slide right over that edge with her.

Chapter Sixteen

With her body slack from the climax, Rayanne collapsed against Blue, careful not to hurt his shoulder. Even though he didn't seem to be feeling any pain, she didn't want to take the risk of making his injury worse.

Especially since she'd just done that to their situation.

This would complicate things and therefore make things worse. No doubt about it. But she hadn't been able to resist Blue five months ago, and she hadn't had any luck resisting him now. Under normal circumstances, that wouldn't have been such a bad thing, but this was far from normal.

She eased off his lap, dropping onto her back, only to remember she wasn't exactly in buck-naked shape. Rayanne reached to pull the covers over her, but Blue stopped her.

"I'm guessing you're not trying to cover up because you're cold," he mumbled, then lowered his head and kissed her belly. Just like that, it rebuilt the heat that she thought had been quenched.

For at least an hour or two, anyway.

"Not cold," she agreed. "But not sure I feel comfortable with my body being sprawled out in front of you."

"Well, you should. You look amazing." He kissed her

again and gave her one of those melting looks, and Rayanne had to fight not to be seduced all over again.

She pulled the quilt over her and sat up, hoping she wouldn't feel so, well, vulnerable, but that feeling apparently didn't have anything to do with nudity. She still felt it when she looked at Blue.

Who was the true definition of looking amazing.

Rayanne sighed. "It'd be so much easier if you were ugly or if I just hated you."

He chuckled, pulled her back to him so that she was in the crook of his good arm. "It'd be so much easier if we were in love."

She frowned, stared up at him.

"You know what I mean," he went on. "You don't trust people because of your father's abandonment, and I don't love because I don't think I deserve it."

That got her attention. "What do you mean?"

He ran his fingers over the small pinholes on his vest. "When my father was alive, he rarely took off this vest. Even when it needed to be cleaned, he'd wait for it at the dry cleaner's. He called it his good-luck charm."

"So do you," she said.

Blue nodded. "I was always begging him to let me wear it to school to show everyone the badge, and one day he gave in." He paused, swallowed hard. "And that's the day that two methheads gunned him down."

Rayanne shook her head. It crushed her heart to think of the pain Blue must have gone through, even if it had happened all those years ago.

"You do know that wasn't your fault and the vest had nothing to do with it?" she asked.

"I know it here." He tapped his head. "Not so much here, though." Blue tapped his heart.

"Kid logic doesn't have to make sense," he added when her mouth tightened a little. "You keep me at a distance because of your father, but I do the same thing. I'm afraid if I care that much for someone again, then… Well, you get what I mean."

Every word.

But where did that leave them? Unable to trust or risk a commitment.

Where did it leave their baby?

"We'll work it all out," he said as if reading her mind, and dropped another kiss on her mouth just as the landline phone on her nightstand beeped.

Since the beep meant someone in the house was trying to reach her, Rayanne slid over a very naked Blue to answer it.

"It's me," Rosalie said. "Woody Janson called here asking to speak to Blue. I've got him on hold for now, but do you want me to put the call through to your room?"

Obviously, Blue was still close enough to hear, because he answered, "Yes," and took the phone. Rayanne moved right next to him so she could hear what Woody had to say.

"Start explaining," Blue snapped the moment Woody came on the line. "What happened to you after you left the ranch, and why are you calling on this line?"

"Wasn't sure your cell was safe. I still haven't been able to prove Caleb's innocent, and I didn't want to take the risk that he was monitoring your phone with a tap. I figured you wouldn't have let him in the house to do the same to the landlines."

No, they hadn't let Caleb inside. Woody, either. Yet the attacks had still happened.

"Did you kill Ace Butler?" Blue came right out and asked.

"Yeah. He took a shot at me. I returned fire, and I hit him. He escaped in a car he had parked nearby. If what I just found out is true, Ace made his way to the hospital where he died."

"He did," Blue verified. "Gandy's dead, too."

"I heard. I hope you don't think I'm all torn up about either Ace's or Gandy's death. They were scum."

"They were," Blue readily admitted, "but what I want to know is did you have anything to do with the attack that left Gandy dead? Because it could have left Rayanne, her family, the ranch hands and me dead, too."

"No, of course not. I wasn't responsible for that." Woody paused, huffed. "Look, I know I'm not exactly high on the list of people you trust, but I want the same thing that you do. My name completely cleared and the person behind these attacks stopped."

Judging from Blue's narrowed eyes, he had some doubts about Woody's innocence. So did she.

"I found out something else," Woody went on a moment later. "I've spent the last half hour trying to verify it, but no luck so far. Still, I thought you'd want to know what I heard from criminal informants."

"I'm listening," Blue assured him.

"I think someone might try to set an explosive device in or near the county jail."

Oh, mercy. Rayanne's heart skipped a beat. "My mother," she managed to say. She scrambled out of the bed, located her jeans on the floor and took out her phone.

"I want details," Blue demanded from Woody.

"Sorry, I don't have them, but I've been monitoring some taps I have in place on two criminal informants, and they were definitely discussing a bomb. I can't verify if they were doing that to find out if I was listening. In other words, a test. Or if the threat's real."

Rayanne's hands were shaking so hard that it took her several tries to press Seth's number, and her brother answered on the first ring.

"Is Mom all right?" Rayanne immediately asked. Blue ended his call with Woody and hurried to her side. "Is there really a bomb threat at the county jail?"

"I don't want you to panic," Seth answered.

Which, of course, made her want to do just that. "There's really a bomb?"

"Maybe. Someone called in a bomb threat, and Mom and the other nine prisoners are being moved to another part of the building. The bomb squad's on the way."

She could tell Seth was trying to keep his voice calm. For her sake, no doubt. But Rayanne could also hear the fear and the concern.

"I don't trust Sheriff Aiden Braddock," Rayanne said. "If something goes wrong, I figure our mother is the last person he'd bother to protect."

Especially since Jewell was charged with murdering the sheriff's father.

"I'm down in Floresville," Seth explained. "I was trying to get a lead on the person who tried to bribe the doctor. I'm heading to Clay Ridge right now."

Rayanne shook her head. "It'll take nearly two hours for you to get there. That's not soon enough if this is some kind of setup to hurt Mom."

"No," Seth said. "You're not going. Is Blue there?"

"I'm here," Blue verified.

"Even if you have to hog-tie her, don't let her go. I'm calling now to find some agents that I trust to work this." And with that, Seth hung up.

Rayanne didn't waste a second getting to her feet, and she started to get dressed. Blue did, too, but he moved right in front of her, forcing eye contact.

"You heard what your brother said," Blue reminded her. "And I agree. You're not going to that jail."

Everything inside was spinning so fast that it was hard to think. "I have to do something."

"Yeah. You have to wait here. Seth will have a team in place soon."

Maybe not soon enough. "This could be a way of getting back at me. At us," she corrected. "If so, Wendell could be behind it."

Blue nodded, continued to dress. "And it could be a ruse to get you to panic. If it is, Caleb or Woody could be behind it. Both of them have access to criminal informants who could have faked this kind of info."

He was right, and Rayanne forced herself to consider that. Still...

"Finish dressing," Blue said. "Then we'll go downstairs and wait for some news."

Despite Seth's and Blue's orders for her to stay put, Rayanne was still debating what to do when Blue brushed his hand over her stomach. It was one of those reminders that she didn't necessarily want.

But needed.

The deputy sheriff in her wanted to go racing to the jail, but the baby had to come first.

Blue leaned in, kissed her. "We'll talk about that later." He tipped his head to the heap of rumpled covers on the bed.

Yes, the heat between them and their apparent inability to fall in love. However, Rayanne was pretty sure that for her, it was no longer an inability.

She was falling in love with Blue—again.

That made her either stupid…human…or both. She was still debating that, too, when there was a knock at the door, and the knob rattled.

"Rayanne?" Rosalie called out.

"She probably heard about the bomb threat," Blue mumbled, and he opened the door.

Rayanne got ready to give Rosalie the same reassurance that Blue and Seth had just given her. But after one look at her sister's face, Rayanne knew a mere reassurance wasn't going to help. There were tears spilling down Rosalie's cheeks.

"The deputy from Clay Ridge just called," Rosalie said, her words rushing together. "A bomb went off at the jail." She paused, swallowed hard. "Mom's been hurt."

BLUE CURSED. NOT JUST because Jewell had been injured but because he knew there was nothing that could stop Rayanne from going to her.

Still, he tried.

"Wait." He caught on to her and turned back to Rosalie. "How bad are her injuries?"

Rosalie shook her head. "The deputy couldn't say. There's an ambulance on the way to take her and the rest of the wounded inmates to the hospital in Clay Ridge."

"I have to see her," Rayanne said, shaking off Blue's grip. She grabbed her holster and gun from the dresser.

Blue darted out into the hall, cutting her off before she could get far. "You should wait until I've had a chance to make some calls."

"You can do that on the drive over." Rayanne looked up at him, and he saw the tears shimmering in her eyes. "What would you do if it was your father who was hurt? And let's take that one step further. What if your father was hurt, and the people around him hated him enough to let him die?"

Oh, man. He'd been afraid she was going to toss that at him. Because it was a darn good argument. If his dad had been hurt, nothing would have stopped him from going.

That meant since he couldn't talk her out of going to Clay Ridge, Blue had to do anything and everything to keep Rayanne safe.

"Who's here at the ranch?" Blue asked Rosalie, following both women down the stairs.

"Roy and the hands, of course. Colt had to go back into town to work."

Not good. The ranch hands had done well so far, but Blue wanted law enforcement for this. "Call Cooper and see if he can arrange for someone to escort Rayanne and me to the hospital so she can see her mother."

Rosalie gave a shaky nod and made the call while they hurried to the kitchen. Roy was there, buckling up a waist holster. Obviously, he was aware that the explosion and Jewell's injuries could be some kind of trap to draw them out into the open.

"I'm going with you," the man insisted.

"Me, too," Rosalie added the moment she finished her call. "Cooper said Colt and Reed are on their way over to escort us to the hospital."

"We can wait for them at the end of the road," Rayanne mumbled. "And they'd better hurry."

Again, Blue had to step in front of Rayanne to stop

her from bolting out the door. "I need to make sure it's safe enough to go out there."

"I'll do that," Roy insisted.

Damn. He was just as stubborn as his daughter. Blue didn't get a chance to argue with the man, because his phone rang, and he saw Seth's name on the screen.

"I'm guessing all of you are headed to Clay Ridge," Seth said the moment Blue answered.

"Even hog-tying won't stop them."

Seth mumbled some profanity. "I'll see what I can do about getting you some help. It's a forty-five-minute drive, and a lot of bad things can happen along the way." He paused. "Is Rayanne listening?"

"No." And Blue moved slightly away from her because he figured this was something Seth didn't want her to hear.

"I just found out from someone in the ambulance that Mom's injuries could be pretty bad," Seth explained.

"Oh, God," Rayanne said, and Blue knew then that she'd heard her brother after all. She snatched the phone from Blue and put it on speaker.

"How bad?" Rayanne demanded.

It took several seconds for Seth to answer. "She's unconscious, has lost plenty of blood and will likely need surgery. That doesn't mean I want you going off—"

That got Rayanne heading out the door again. She punched the end-call button and tossed him his phone, and all Blue could do was draw his gun to help Roy make sure the yard was clear.

Rayanne opened the door of an SUV that was parked close to the house and would have gotten behind the wheel if Roy hadn't stopped her. "I'll drive," her father insisted. "That way, the two of you can keep watch."

"Me, too," Rosalie said, and that was when Blue realized she'd also grabbed a gun.

"I guess it won't do any good to say just how bad an idea this is," Blue grumbled.

Nope.

No good whatsoever.

The best Blue could do was maneuver Rayanne and Rosalie into the backseat so he could ride shotgun. Rayanne got behind Blue. Rosalie behind her father.

"Both of you stay down," Blue warned them.

Whether they would was anyone's guess, but at least Rosalie slid lower as Roy took off.

"It'll take Colt and Reed at least another ten minutes to get out here," Roy said to no one in particular.

"Drive slow," Blue advised him.

The sooner they met up with the deputies, the better, and Blue wanted to minimize their time on the road without the added protection. Since it was already dark, their attacker might be able to hide somewhere along the way.

"I'll call the Clay Ridge hospital," Rosalie volunteered, "and see if there's an update."

Blue needed to start his own calls. The big one had already been made—Colt and Reed were on the way—but he wanted to know the location of their three suspects. And also how someone had managed to set off a bomb in the county jail. He took out his phone to get started just as Roy brought the SUV to a stop at the end of the road.

"We'll wait for Reed and Colt," Roy said. "As soon as they show, we'll all head out together."

Rayanne opened her mouth, no doubt to protest that, but Roy shot her a look that only a father could have managed. Yeah, Rayanne was hardheaded but Roy made it clear that arguing wasn't going to make him budge.

Blue kept his gun drawn, and he kept watch while he made the first call to Agent Hale at the ATF. The county sheriff had likely already arranged for a CSI team, but Blue wanted to get some federal agents on the scene.

"Headlights," Roy pointed out, and he tipped his head to the vehicle approaching.

"I'll make sure it's Colt and Reed," Rayanne said, taking out her phone again. "And if it is, hit the gas and let's get out of here."

Blue's call to Hale went to voice mail, and he put away his phone, his attention planted on those headlights. He wouldn't breathe easier until he had confirmation from Rayanne that it was backup and not someone else ready to attack them.

"It's them," Rayanne relayed several moments later.

Roy pulled out onto the main road, Colt and Reed right behind them, and as Rayanne had said, her father hit the accelerator.

Just as a fireball exploded right in front of them.

Chapter Seventeen

The blast shook the entire SUV, and it took Rayanne a moment to realize what had happened.

Someone had detonated a bomb.

Roy slammed on the brakes, and despite the fact all of them were wearing seat belts, the jolt threw them forward. She hcard Blue make a sharp sound of pain, no doubt because the seat belt had caught his shoulder.

"Back up," Blue practically shouted to Roy. "Get us out of here."

Rayanne saw that Colt was already doing that. His tires screamed against the asphalt, and the cruiser sped backward, giving them enough distance for Roy to do the same.

But he didn't get far.

The second blast came at them like a thunderbolt, tearing through the road in the meager space between the cruiser and their SUV. Blue cursed, reached over the seat and pushed Rosalie and her down.

Rayanne had already drawn her gun, but she got it ready in case she had a chance to fire and stop this monster from setting off another explosive.

Blue had been right. The bombing at the jail had likely been designed to draw them out into the open. And it'd worked. But her mother was hurt. Maybe dying. There was no way she could have stayed put and not gone to the hospital.

Now that decision might cost all of them their lives.

Blue's phone rang, and he hit the speaker button. "Are you all right?" she heard Colt ask.

Blue glanced at each of them. "I think so. You see anyone, anything?"

"Nothing.... Wait, maybe something. Look to the driver's side of the SUV."

Rayanne lifted her head to do just that, but all she could see was a cloud of milky-gray smoke caused by the bombs. She knew there were woods on that side of the road. There were pastures on the side they were on. It would make sense that if their attacker wanted to hide, he would use the woods.

"I don't see anyone," Blue told Colt. "How many and how close?"

"I only got a glimpse of one man, and he ducked behind the trees."

If it was the same guy who'd fired at the house earlier, then he could be carrying a rifle and use it to rip the SUV apart with bullets.

That kicked up her heartbeat a significant notch. They had to do something to get out of there alive.

"How bad's the road?" Roy asked. "Can I drive around the damage?"

"Probably not," Colt answered.

Rayanne groaned. If they couldn't move, then it meant they were trapped just waiting for the next attack. And she figured it wouldn't take long for that next attack to come.

"I'm going to try to use the shoulder to turn around

and get us out of here," Roy said. "You keep an eye on the guy you spotted."

"Will do," Colt assured him.

Roy put the SUV in gear, and while Blue and Rayanne kept watch, he maneuvered the vehicle off the asphalt and onto the narrow dirt shoulder. Thankfully, there'd been no recent rains, or both the shoulder and the ditch would have been a bog. Roy was able to gain enough traction to make some progress in getting them turned around.

"Why hasn't he finished us off?" Blue mumbled.

That caused the skin to crawl on the back of her neck, and it was a question she should have already asked herself. For nearly a minute, their attacker had had them at a standstill, and it would have been the perfect time to kill them. Probably Reed and Colt, too, since they would have tried to stop it.

So why were they all still alive?

"This is a kidnapping," Rayanne said.

Blue nodded.

Just as there was a plinging sound as something hit the front of the SUV. A split second later, there was another one.

"Tear gas," Blue and she said in unison.

They didn't have to wait long for confirmation of that. The wispy gas immediately started to spew from the canisters. Their windows were all closed, but the gas seeped through, and they all started to cough.

"He wants us out of the SUV so he can take us at gunpoint," Blue told Roy.

Yes, and then do heaven-knew-what to them.

If it was Caleb or Woody behind this, then they might want to use Blue and her as pawns in whatever dirty dealings they were into. Or maybe they would use her to force

Blue into helping them cover up the plot that landed those confiscated weapons back into the hands of criminals.

And if it was Wendell, then they could be pawns for a different reason.

To punish her mother.

Of course, this could be Gandy's men, carrying out his wishes from beyond the grave. It didn't matter that Gandy was already dead. He could have set this into motion, knowing that he would finally get his revenge against Blue for his investigation.

Despite the fact he was coughing and wheezing as much as the rest of them, Roy kept maneuvering the SUV. He didn't panic and gun the engine; he inched forward, then back, until he had enough room to get the vehicle around the crater in the road and onto the shoulder.

He hit the accelerator.

"I can't see," Roy said through his coughs.

Neither could Rayanne. The tear gas was burning like fire in her eyes, and she was coughing so hard that she couldn't catch her breath. She prayed this wouldn't do anything to harm the baby.

"Stay on the shoulder as long as you can," Colt warned him. "The road might not be stable."

Roy did. The SUV bobbed over the uneven surface of the grass-and-dirt shoulder, and thanks to the night breeze clearing away some of the smoke, Rayanne got just a glimpse of the massive hole in the road. If Roy had gone into that, they would have been stuck again.

"Keep moving," Colt instructed. "Let's get back to the ranch so we can regroup."

And she could check on her mother. Even now, that was pressing as hard on her as this nightmarish situation. If this monster had managed to kill her mother, then whoever he was, he would pay.

Roy finally maneuvered around the massive hole, and Rayanne spotted Colt's cruiser. For the first time since this ordeal had started, she thought maybe they might finally make it out of there.

But she was wrong.

A bullet crashed into the SUV.

"GET DOWN!" BLUE SHOUTED, mainly to Rayanne.

As a deputy, she no doubt had the instinct to try to return fire, but he didn't want her taking a bullet while trying to protect the rest of them.

Roy hit the gas, but another bullet ripped through the windshield and shattered the safety glass. Mixed with the lingering smoke from the explosives and the tear gas, it made it nearly impossible to see.

Worse, the bullets just kept coming.

Not inside the vehicle, though. Now that the windshield was gone, the shooter was aiming at the tires.

Trying to stop them.

Worse, there wasn't just one shooter. There were likely several of them, and they seemed to be stretched out in the woods, firing nonstop as Roy drove past them. If so, then this was a well-orchestrated attack by someone who was desperate to get their hands on Rayanne and him.

"Get off the road," Blue instructed Roy. "Go through the fence and into the pasture."

Of course, there were no guarantees gunmen weren't waiting there, too, but at least the pasture was wide-open, and Blue had a chance of picking off one of these idiots if they came out of cover.

Blue risked glancing back at Rayanne to make sure she was okay.

She wasn't.

Both she and her sister were pale and shaking, but at least they were alive and unharmed. And thank God, they were actually staying down on the seat as he'd told them to do.

It crushed his heart to think of what this was doing to her and the baby. To Rosalie and Roy, too. He was an agent, had been in the middle of gunfire before, and while that never would be routine, the others had to be terrified.

Heck, Blue was, too.

And later he'd kick himself for allowing things to get this far. If there was a later, that is.

"Hold on," Roy said.

Rayanne's father gave the steering wheel a sharp turn to the left and accelerated even more so they'd clear the ditch. It worked, but it wasn't a smooth landing.

Far from it.

The SUV bolted through the wooden fence and sent a spray of debris right at them and tearing through what was left of the windshield. A thick piece of wood smacked against Blue's arm, and he could have sworn he saw stars. He forced aside the pain, not easy to do, and got ready for another attack.

He didn't have to wait long.

The bullets started again. Nonstop. All of them tearing into the lower part of the SUV. There wouldn't be much of the tires left by now, but he hoped it was enough to get them the heck out of there.

Roy hit the gas again, but the SUV didn't move. The flat tires just spun around in the soft ground. They were stuck. *Again.* Sitting ducks with their attackers closing in on them.

"Colt, I can't move," Roy shouted toward the phone, though he kept trying to get the SUV out of the bog. "Anything you can do?"

"It's too risky for you to come out on the road to get to me. I'm coming closer," Blue heard Colt answer over the thick blasts. "The cruiser's bullet resistant, so I'm going to try and get behind you and push your vehicle to get it moving."

That would put Rayanne's brother and Reed in the direct path of those bullets. Still, it might save Rayanne and the baby from being hit, and right now Blue had to put their safety above all others'. However, he did have to wonder how Roy felt about his youngest son taking the brunt of the danger on his shoulders.

"If I get stuck, too," Colt added, "Cooper and some of the ranch hands are on the way out here. Just hold your positions until we can fight off these idiots."

Blue hoped they wouldn't have to fight much longer. Each bullet fired was a risk that one of them could get hurt or killed.

It didn't take long for Colt to come crashing through the fence. The shots kept coming, but as he'd said he would do, Colt turned the cruiser, lining up the front end of it with the back bumper of the SUV. Blue heard Colt rev his engine and could feel the cruiser pushing against the SUV.

But nothing happened.

Colt tried again. And again. Still nothing.

"Hang on," Colt warned them a split second before he hit his accelerator. The cruiser bashed into them.

The jolt caused Blue's pain to spike again, but it would

have been well worth it if it'd worked. It hadn't. Roy cursed when the SUV still didn't budge.

"I'll pull up beside you," Colt finally said. "I want all of you to climb into the cruiser."

Blue didn't care for the idea of Rayanne being outside for even a second or two, but he couldn't see another way out of this. Cooper and the others wouldn't be able to get close, not with the bullets flying, so escape in the cruiser might be their best bet.

Colt pulled up on the driver's side of the SUV, and he aligned the cruiser's back door with the SUV.

"Go," Roy said, motioning toward Rosalie since she was the nearest to the cruiser.

Rosalie gave a shaky nod, and with a firm grip on her gun, she opened the back door of the cruiser. The moment she was in, she scrambled to the side, motioning for Rayanne to follow her.

Despite the roar of the bullets, Rayanne hesitated. She was no doubt thinking a jolt like that could harm the baby. And it could. But staying put could do the same.

"Just take it as easy as you can," Blue told her.

Her gaze met his, and even in the darkness he could see the raw emotion in her eyes. Emotions that Rayanne rarely allowed anyone to see.

"You'll be right behind me," she said, and it wasn't a question. More like an order.

"I promise."

But the words had no sooner left his mouth than there was a flash of headlights behind them. The driver had on the high beams, and with the wisps of smoke still stirring around, it made it hard for Blue to see.

However, he could make out two men leaning out of the car windows. Both were armed.

And the car was headed across the pasture right toward them.

Chapter Eighteen

Rayanne got only a glimpse of the gunmen before Blue pushed her back down on the seat. It wasn't a second too soon, because the men started firing.

Not from a distance like before.

These shots were deafening, and they were no longer aiming at the tires. These ripped through the roof of the SUV. If the men were trying to scare them, it was working.

At least, it did for a few seconds.

Then the anger slammed through her. These idiots were putting all of them at risk—including the baby—and for what? Rayanne wished she could grab one of them and demand answers.

Since the SUV door was still open, Rayanne could see Rosalie on the backseat of the cruiser. She had a gun, but like her, Rosalie was having to stay down, too, since some of those shots were coming much too close to her.

So far the back windshield of the cruiser was holding, but it might not for long. It was bullet resistant, but eventually enough shots might be able to tear through it.

Roy threw open his door, positioning it so that it was aligned with the cruiser's door. It would give them a little more protection if they jumped to the cruiser. Still, Rayanne was worried about what could be a hard fall and the seconds that she'd be in the open. She and the baby would be a clean target for those bullets.

"Move over," Roy told Rosalie. "Get on the floor."

The moment her sister did that, Roy threw himself onto the backseat. Well, the edge of it, anyway. He was taking a huge risk by not staying behind cover.

And he was doing it for her.

Rayanne realized that when he motioned for her to jump. He was going to catch her while using his body to shield her.

"Do it," Blue said. "Now!"

She wanted to jump. But wanted Blue to be safe, too, and in that split second of hesitation, Rayanne heard a sound she didn't want to hear.

More tear gas came at them, the metal canister bouncing onto the SUV.

Everything seemed to happen at once. Roy reached for her, but the jolt sent him flying back. Not a jolt from the tear gas. This was another explosion, and the blinding white light from it flashed on the side of the SUV.

The blast vibrated through her body, pounding in her ears while the tear gas blistered her eyes. The coughing started again. Not just for her but for all of them.

And that wasn't the worst of their problems.

She figured those gunmen would soon be out of their vehicle and on their way to take them.

Or kill them.

"Go!" she managed to shout out to Colt. "Leave now!"

At least that way, Rosalie would be safe. Colt, Reed and her father, too.

But Colt didn't leave.

Instead he threw the cruiser into reverse and positioned it between their attackers and the SUV.

"I'm getting Rayanne out of here," Blue said to Colt through the phone. And that was the only warning Rayanne got before he took hold of her.

"Come on," Blue said to her in a whisper. He shoved his phone in his pocket, crawled over the seat and maneuvered her out the door.

"Try to stay quiet," Blue added. "They can't see us. And this is our best chance of getting out of here."

Staying quiet was next to impossible because of the coughing, but at least the combined sounds of the engines helped drown it out. Maybe it'd help enough for all of them to get to safety.

Blue didn't lead her toward the cruiser. Instead they headed toward the fence that fronted the ranch road.

"Rosalie," she said in a rough whisper. Rayanne didn't want to leave her sister back there.

"Colt will get her out," Blue promised.

Rayanne prayed that was true. Colt had put himself, Roy and Rosalie in danger to save Blue and her, and she hoped that didn't cost any of them their lives.

"Keep moving," Blue mumbled.

She did. There was no turning back now. Even when the shots started again, Rayanne knew she had no choice but to keep moving.

The fence was a good twenty yards away, but if Blue and she reached it, they'd have decent cover between the fence and the ditch. Plus, they wouldn't be that far from Tucker's house, and they could duck inside until Cooper and the others could make it to them.

Each step was a challenge. Mainly because her legs were shaking, and it felt as if someone had her heart and lungs in a vise. But each step also took them farther away from the tear-gas fog. The coughing faded, and Rayanne focused just on getting to safety.

Behind them the pace of the shots picked up. Not just from one gun, either. It sounded as if several different weapons were being fired. Maybe from Colt and Reed. If so, that could mean they were in the middle of another gunfight.

The moment they reached the fence, Blue hooked his arm around her to hoist her up onto the rungs. As a kid, she'd climbed this fence dozens of times, but it suddenly felt a mile high.

She glanced over her shoulder, hoping to see Colt's cruiser racing away from the tangle of smoke and vehicles. But it wasn't. Worse, those shots were still coming.

"We have to help them," Rayanne insisted.

"I will. Once I get you to safety."

Rayanne was about to argue with that, but a sound stopped her.

Footsteps.

Not coming from behind them but directly in front of them. Both Blue and she automatically took aim in that direction but didn't fire in case it was family or one of the ranch hands.

It wasn't.

"I wouldn't move if I were you," the man said.

It took Rayanne a moment to pick through the darkness and find him. Wearing dark clothes, he looked like a shadow when he glanced out from the side of Tucker's house.

Blue pulled her to the ground and fired at the mystery man, but the guy had already taken cover.

"Like I said, I wouldn't move if I were you," the man

repeated, not leaving the cover of the house. "You're both belly-down on some explosive devices, and if you so much as wiggle your toes, you'll be blown to bits."

BLUE AUTOMATICALLY FROZE.

He hadn't felt anything unusual when he'd dropped to the ground, but that didn't mean a bomb wasn't close enough to do some serious damage.

Of course, this could be yet another part of the ruse to get them to stay put.

If Rayanne and he didn't fight back, then they'd likely be kidnapped or harmed in some way. Because if this clown had wanted them dead, he would have already fired the shots to make that happen.

So what the heck was going on here?

Blue checked over his shoulder to make sure they weren't about to be ambushed from behind.

No one was anywhere near them.

But in the pasture he could see Colt driving the cruiser away from the stuck SUV. Rayanne's brother wasn't coming toward them but rather headed to the back of the pasture, and there were gunmen in pursuit.

Maybe Colt would manage to get Rosalie and the others to safety, but it was obvious Colt had his hands full. And Blue couldn't wait on Cooper and the ranch hands to come to their aid. He had to do something to get Rayanne and the baby to safety, too.

"What should we do?" Rayanne whispered.

Her voice was shaking a little, just enough for him to hear the fear in her voice. However, she had a firm lawman's grip on her gun, and she had it pointed directly at the man behind Tucker's house.

Blue looked around, still didn't spot an explosive, but

the man did have a gun trained on them. If they moved, he might feel compelled to start shooting. What Blue needed to do was figure out a way to defuse this situation or else wait until the guy left cover so he'd have a decent shot.

"What do you want?" Blue demanded from the man.

"Me? I don't want nothing. Well, other than for you to stay right where you are. Pretty soon you'll be somebody else's problem and not mine."

Even though the guy stayed hidden, Blue saw him mumble something and lean in toward his collar. No doubt where he had some kind of communication device.

"Someone else?" Blue repeated.

"The person who hired me to do this, and before you ask, I don't know who he is. Personally, I'd like to keep it that way. Knowing that kind of stuff can make a person a loose end."

Yeah, it could, especially if it was a federal agent trying to cover up his part in a string of felonies.

"Are you the one who took shots at us at the ranch?" Blue asked. He purposely kept his voice low, hoping the idiot would lean out from cover to better hear him.

He didn't.

The man stayed put. "Yeah," he finally answered. "Nothing personal."

"A man died," Blue reminded him.

"Still don't make it personal."

Blue had hoped he would just keep yakking, because it might help him figure out who was behind this. Plus, it might distract him enough for Blue to get off a shot.

"Someone's coming," Rayanne whispered. She tipped her head to the end of the ranch road. No headlights. But there was a dark vehicle creeping its way toward them.

"Cooper, maybe?" Blue asked.

"No. I don't recognize the car."

Now what? Blue didn't figure this was good news for Rayanne and him, since this was likely the "someone else" that the bozo had mentioned earlier.

And that someone else might have a different notion about keeping Rayanne and him alive.

"Stay down," Blue whispered to her.

"What are you planning to do?" Rayanne immediately snapped.

"First I'm going to try to shoot the guy hiding behind the house, and then you'll roll in the ditch so I can try to deal with whoever's in that car."

Even with just the moonlight, he could see the disapproval on her face. "And if there's really an explosive device?"

"That's why I want you to roll into the ditch. I'll cover you as best I can." Which he hoped was enough to keep Rayanne from being hurt.

"We don't have time to debate this," Blue reminded her, and tipped his head to the vehicle that was now only about twenty yards away.

"Y'all better not be thinking about doing anything stupid," the man warned them.

But Blue was already past the point of thinking about it. He took aim.

And fired.

The second the thick blast rang out, Rayanne went toward the ditch.

No explosion, thank God.

Blue held his breath, praying, and he got off another shot before he rolled in front of her. Both his shots missed, but it brought the man out from cover so he could return fire. Blue pulled the trigger again.

This time, he didn't miss.

"Move," Blue told Rayanne. He wanted to put as much distance between them and the approaching vehicle as he could.

But they didn't get far.

They'd made it only a few inches when both the front passenger's- and driver's-side doors opened. Two armed men jumped out, and they pointed their weapons right at Rayanne and him.

"Move and you die," one of the goons said. Both were heavily armed and were wearing bulletproof vests.

"I've heard that before," Blue snarled. "Heard there were explosives beneath us, too. That turned out to be a lie, didn't it?"

A lie Blue wished he'd figured out sooner so he could have maybe gotten Rayanne out of there.

If the man had any reaction to that, he didn't show it. He mumbled something into the grape-sized communicator clipped on his collar. "Drop your weapons, put your hands in the air and get up," he ordered. "Then walk slowly toward the car."

Blue huffed. "And why would we do that? You'll just gun us down."

"My boss doesn't want you dead," he assured them. Coming from him, it was no assurance at all, of course.

"Really?" Blue asked. He adjusted his position so that he was between Rayanne and the gunmen. "Because I'm getting the feeling that death is on the agenda here."

The goon had another mumbled conversation with the person on the other end of the communicator, and he glanced up the road, where there was another car coming toward them. He didn't react by turning his gun in that direction, which meant this wasn't a threat. It could be yet more hired guns.

"We can go ahead and shoot McCurdy," the man said to his partner the moment the second car pulled to a stop.

"No!" Rayanne shouted. And she would have scrambled in front of him if Blue hadn't stopped her.

"Why'd your boss change his mind?" Blue demanded. He got ready for the worst. If the bullets started flying, he'd just have to throw himself over Rayanne and pray that he got off the right shots before these two killed him.

There was more whispered conversation on the communicator. "He says he's getting tired of waiting for Miss McKinnon to cooperate."

"And why should I?" she fired back.

"Because it'll save McCurdy and you'll get to see your mother."

Blue heard her pull in a breath. "My mother?" she mumbled.

"You've got five seconds, Miss McKinnon," the man said, motioning with his gun.

Thank heaven Rayanne didn't make a move, but Blue braced himself for the fight that was about to come.

However, before the five seconds ticked off, the back door of the second car flew open, and someone stepped out.

"Either get in the car now," he growled, "or your mother and both of you die."

Chapter Nineteen

Rayanne glared at the man who'd just threatened them.

Wendell.

He glared right back at her, and she saw the sheer anger on his face that was no doubt mirrored on her own.

"You hurt my mother," Rayanne managed to say. Not easily. It felt as if someone had hold of her throat—her heart, too—making it hard to speak.

Blue tried to step in front of her. Trying to protect her as he'd done over and over again since this nightmare had begun. But Rayanne held her ground. She wanted to hear what this piece of slime had to say, and she wanted to look him in the eyes when he said it.

"What happened to Jewell was an accident," Wendell said as if it excused everything. "I wanted her very much alive and aware of what was going on, but the idiot who set the explosives didn't do a good job. He'll pay for that."

It tightened her throat even more to hear Wendell admit it aloud. It didn't matter that her mother wasn't supposed to have been hurt. She had been.

And Wendell would pay for that.

"The explosives were only meant to draw you out," Wendell added. He sat down on the edge of the backseat. "No one was supposed to have been hurt."

"Well, they were. Your hired gun could have killed the sheriff, your own grandson," Blue pointed out. Like her, he sounded as if he barely had a choke hold on the anger boiling inside him.

Blue's reminder turned Wendell's jaw to iron. "Like I said, he'll pay for his mistake. Just like Jewell will for killing my son."

Wendell glanced around him, no doubt looking for any signs that Cooper, Colt and the others were approaching.

And they would be.

The question was, would they get there in time to stop Wendell from kidnapping Blue and her?

"I know what you're thinking," Wendell said, his mouth bent into a near smile. "That your brothers or daddy will come to the rescue. Well, that's why we're waiting out here. For a little while, anyway."

"You want them dead," she mumbled.

"All of them. And I figure you're a delicious little piece of bait standing out here like this."

Sweet heaven. He was right. Despite the bad blood between Roy, her brothers and her, Roy had already tried to save her once tonight, and he would no doubt try to do it again.

"Killing Roy won't get back at Jewell," she tried.

Wendell lifted his shoulder. "You're wrong about that." He studied her, smiled. "Oh, you didn't know they've been chatting regularly. Ever since your sister's baby was stolen."

"I knew," she lied. "But conversations don't mean anything. After all, we're having one now, and that hardly means we're on friendly terms."

Even in the moonlight, she saw the anger flash in his

eyes. Wendell wanted only to hurt and didn't want to hear logic.

"Disarm them," Wendell snapped to his two goons. "Then get them inside the car."

Rayanne didn't budge and knew that if she got in, neither she nor Blue would be alive much longer.

"You intend to kill us to punish my mother," Rayanne said. She stepped to Blue's side, despite his attempts to stop her, and she slid her hand over her stomach.

She'd never used the baby card, but she would now. She would do whatever it took to survive so that her precious baby could survive, too.

"You really think you can kill a pregnant woman?" she demanded.

Wendell kept tossing her glares while he continued to keep watch around them. He didn't seem to notice the men making their way across the pasture, coming from the direction of the ranch house.

Cooper? Maybe some of the hands. Whoever they were, Rayanne hoped she could distract Wendell long enough for someone to get off a shot and send this monster to his maker.

Of course, it could be more of Wendell's hired guns out there, too, but Rayanne couldn't let her thoughts go there. Blue and she had to survive this for the sake of their baby, and while they were surviving, she had to make sure Wendell didn't take out anyone else to quench his need for revenge.

"I can do whatever it takes to avenge my son's murder," Wendell answered. "Besides, losing a grandchild will make the cut even deeper for Jewell."

And there it was, all spelled out for her. Rayanne

hadn't thought for one minute that she could actually negotiate with Wendell, but now she was sure.

"If you're going to kill us, anyway," she said, "then we might as well die on McKinnon land. You, too. Because I figure Blue and I can get off a shot before your men take us out. One shot's all we'll need to make sure you're dead."

The corner of Wendell's mouth lifted. "You always were a scrappy one. I'm sure Jewell will take it especially hard when she finds out you've been murdered."

"If Jewell lives," Blue tossed out there. "This could all be for no reason. That probably leaves a bitter taste in your mouth, huh?"

The two goons tightened their grips on their weapons, obviously waiting for their boss to give the word to put them in the car. That was when Blue and she would need to make their move. Hopefully by then, whoever was in the pasture would be in place to help them.

Wendell didn't respond to Blue's verbal jab. He just made another sweeping look around. Thank God whoever was in the pasture ducked down just in time. So that probably meant it was friend and not foe.

"For someone so hell-bent on wanting us dead," Blue went on, "you saved us by phoning in that there was a bomb in Rayanne's truck."

"I didn't do that. Ruby-Lee did."

Ruby-Lee, his caretaker, who'd been with Wendell when he'd come to the ranch. "Why would she try to help us?" Rayanne asked.

"Because she's a sap, that's why." The disdain was crystal clear in his voice. "She listened in on conversations she shouldn't have and thought one of my men had set the bomb. She figured I didn't know about it or

I would have done something to stop it. *Right*. She tried to stick her nose where it didn't belong, and now she'll pay for that, too."

If the woman wasn't already dead, she soon would be. That was yet another reason to stop this monster and try to rescue the woman who'd saved them.

"Did you set up Caleb and Woody?" Blue asked. Maybe as a distraction ploy so Wendell wouldn't notice the men in the pasture.

Wendell huffed. "Good grief, what does it matter now?"

Blue glared at him. "You did set them up. How?"

"You can hire hackers, good ones, for a lot less than explosives experts. I figured if I could set up the feds, then maybe I could walk away from this clear. But it's too risky. Once you two are dead, that leaves too many McKinnons who might be able to piece things together."

And not just McKinnons but Seth, too. No way would he drop this without getting to the truth.

"Take them to the hospital," Wendell said to the men. "Finish things there and send me photos."

"Photos?" Rayanne and Blue asked in unison.

"You don't think I'd wait around for your brothers to arrest me, do you?" Wendell didn't wait for an answer. "Not a chance. I'm headed out of the country, where I'll be well out of McKinnon reach. All that's left now is the grieving, and if Jewell lives, she'll be doing plenty of that. Because your deaths are just the start. I'll finish all of you off."

And with that death order, Wendell slammed the car door, and his driver hit the accelerator.

He was getting away.

Rayanne wanted to fire into the car to stop him, but she didn't get a chance.

The hired killers came right at Blue and her.

BLUE DIDN'T FIRE when the armed men charged them. Rayanne was still too close, practically right in the line of fire, and if he pulled the trigger, they almost certainly would, too.

Wendell had already given them orders to kill, so it wasn't much of a stretch to believe they would go ahead and murder Rayanne and him right here.

Or rather, try to kill them.

Blue wasn't going to let that happen.

He jumped in front of Rayanne, using his body to block them from getting to her. Both men rammed into him, one hitting his shoulder and nearly knocking the breath right out of Blue.

That didn't stop him.

Blue bashed one of the men on his head with his gun. It caused him to stagger back. Just enough. Blue was able to get off a shot.

The bullet hit the guy squarely in the chest, and even though he was wearing a Kevlar vest, the impact of the shot dropped him like a stone, and he gasped for breath. The injury wouldn't kill him, but it would incapacitate him enough that he wasn't a threat.

Blue hoped.

He kicked the man's gun from his hand and turned to deflect the other goon when he jumped right at him. Blue's gun was out of position to fire.

But Rayanne's wasn't.

She fired, her shot also going into the second man's

chest. She reached down to disarm the man, who was now groaning and clutching his chest, but a sound stopped her.

It was the cruiser, coming from the other end of the ranch road. Colt had obviously managed to circle around. The moment he pulled the cruiser to a stop, both Reed and he jumped out, training their weapons on the men.

"Wendell's the one behind this," Blue said.

"And he's getting away," Rayanne added, already heading for the hired guns' car, probably because it was blocking the road, and the cruiser wouldn't be able to get past it.

Rosalie and Roy got out of the cruiser, aiming their guns at the men on the ground, too, and Blue had to run to catch up with Rayanne.

"Don't you try to stop me," she warned him, and he could tell from that determined look in her eyes that stopping her wasn't even possible. "You know if Wendell gets away, that the attacks won't stop. He'll just keep hiring people to come after us."

Blue cursed. Because it was true.

"Can you handle this?" Blue asked Reed.

The deputy nodded and motioned toward Cooper and some ranch hands who were making their way toward them. "I've got plenty of backup."

Colt nodded and got behind the wheel. Blue took over at shotgun, and Rayanne jumped into the backseat behind her brother. Colt threw the car into reverse and hit the gas while they buckled up.

"Wendell's on his way to the airport," Blue told Colt. "What's the fastest way there?"

"This way," Colt answered the moment they reached the end of the ranch road and turned right. He spun out onto the highway and put the pedal to the metal.

Blue couldn't see Wendell's car, but then, they'd had a head start.

Colt took out his phone and punched in some numbers. "Call the airport," he told whoever answered.

Blue had never been to the airport but knew it was just a small strip, mainly used for private planes and crop dusting. It was likely that Wendell would be the only "customer" at this time of night.

"No answer at the airport," Colt said a few moments later, and he added some profanity. "Either Wendell's paid them off or he's fixed it so they can't answer."

Which could mean he'd had them killed.

It sickened Blue to think of just how far Wendell would go to get back at Jewell. Heaven knew how many lives he'd ended or put in danger, and two of those lives were in the backseat. Blue caught a glimpse of her in the rear-view mirror.

"Hurry," was all she said when their gazes met.

Colt did.

He took the curvy highway as fast as he could and requested backup and roadblocks. Maybe, just maybe, it'd be enough, because Blue didn't want him and Rayanne to live the rest of their lives looking over their shoulders.

"The turn for the airport's just a half mile up on the left," Rayanne told Blue.

Colt probably had no plans to slow down until the last possible second. However, when he rounded a sharp curve, he had to slam on his brakes.

Because Wendell's car was there.

Smack-dab in the middle of the road.

The cruiser's brakes squealed on the asphalt, and Colt turned the steering wheel to avoid a head-on collision and came to a stop.

But before any of them could even take aim, Wendell's driver fired at them through his already-opened window.

The shots blasted into their car, but thankfully, none of them hit them. Unfortunately, the glass cracked and webbed, making it next to impossible to see.

Not good.

Because Wendell's driver stopped firing and hit the gas, no doubt ready to turn the car around and speed away.

"Not this time," Rayanne mumbled. She leaned out the window on the driver's side.

Blue leaned out on his side.

And they both fired.

Not at the car itself, because it was likely bullet resistant. They aimed for the tires before the driver could move.

It was pitch-dark, hardly the best conditions to stop a killer, but Blue and Rayanne kept firing.

Wendell's driver managed to right the angle of the car, and he hit the accelerator again. Colt went in pursuit with Rayanne and Blue still firing.

Within seconds, both the driver and Colt had the vehicles flying down the road.

"Get back in and put on your seat belt," Blue shouted to Rayanne.

She didn't listen. They both fired shots, each of them slamming into the rear windshield of the car. Blue immediately saw the car fishtail, and almost like a swoosh of breath, it left the road.

And slammed into some trees.

Colt hit his brakes, trying to turn the car around so they would have a better shot if Wendell or his driver came out firing.

But they didn't.

The sound of the blast ripped through Wendell's car. A fireball that thundered through the night.

Blue had a split-second realization that there must have been explosives in the vehicle. Another split second to remember that Rayanne was still leaning out the window.

And the fiery debris came right at them.

Chapter Twenty

Rayanne didn't have time to react, but Blue certainly did. He caught on to her and pulled her back inside the car.

It wasn't a second too soon.

A piece of Wendell's car came flying right at her and skidded off the top of their vehicle.

"Get us out of here!" Blue shouted.

Colt did. He hit the gas, and they sped away just as there was a second blast. The impact shook their own car and blew the rest of Wendell's vehicle to smithereens.

"Explosives," Colt mumbled. "I'm betting Wendell hadn't counted on that happening."

No, but Wendell had obviously been using bombs right and left to get to them. They'd been lucky that Wendell and his goons hadn't succeeded. Well, not with them, anyway.

Her mother was a different story.

"We need to get to the hospital," she insisted.

Thankfully, neither Blue nor Colt argued with her. While he continued to drive, Colt took out his phone to make some calls, and Blue climbed over the seat and dropped down next to her. He pulled her into his arms and then checked her over from head to toe.

"Are you okay?" he asked.

"I wasn't hurt," she settled for saying. "You?"

Blue settled for giving her the same lie.

They'd gotten lucky. None of them had been physically hurt, but her mother had been and maybe others. Wendell hadn't cared how many people he involved in his revenge scheme.

"Wendell's dead," she said. No way could he have survived that. Rayanne hadn't been sure how she would feel about that, but she felt only relief. This way, he couldn't hurt her or her family again.

Unless…

"We need to make sure Wendell didn't somehow make it out of the car before it exploded," she mumbled.

Blue nodded and took out his phone, but Colt said something before Blue could dial.

"Reed's taking the two henchmen to jail," Colt relayed to them after he finished his call. "Cooper's getting a CSI team out to the site of Wendell's explosion."

Good.

Rayanne wouldn't breathe easier until she knew for sure.

"I've got a call into the hospital to get an update on Jewell," Colt continued. "Dad's bringing Rosalie to the hospital, too. They're not far behind us."

It had become second nature for Rayanne to scowl anytime Roy was mentioned, but it was hard to scowl at a man who'd tried to save her life.

Ditto for Blue.

Of course, she'd quit scowling at him about the same time they'd landed in bed together. Later they'd need to talk about that and hopefully figure out where to go from here. For now, though, her priority was her mother.

Colt and Blue continued to make calls, each of them

asking for reports and updates. Rayanne considered making one of her own to try to personally speak to a nurse or a doctor at the Clay Ridge hospital, but part of her was terrified of what she might learn.

Her nerves were raw, right at the surface, and with the adrenaline still rocketing through her, she couldn't take any more bad news tonight.

"That was Agent Hale," Blue explained when he finished another call. "He's looking into the possibility that Wendell hired someone to set up Caleb and Woody with those illegal weapons."

"I don't think it's just a possibility," she said. "I'm pretty sure Wendell was telling the truth. In fact, he was bragging about all the criminal things he'd done.... Oh, God. What about Ruby-Lee? He said he was going to have her killed."

"One of the Clay Ridge deputies is on his way to her place now," Colt volunteered.

Rayanne said a quick prayer for the woman. Ruby-Lee had tried to stop a monster and now might have paid for it with her life.

With every muscle in her body rock hard, she was surprised when she felt the little flutters in her stomach. Except this was slightly more than a flutter.

It felt like a kick.

"What's wrong?" Blue immediately asked. "You gasped."

Had she? Rayanne hadn't even noticed, but she took his hand and placed it on her belly. "The baby."

She hadn't expected Blue to be able to feel it, but it was as if the baby wanted to prove a point.

That he or she was alive and well.

The next thump landed right against Blue's palm.

He laughed. It was laced with nerves and fatigue, but it also made her smile.

"Uh, are you two okay?" Colt asked, eyeing them in the rearview mirror.

"Just parent stuff," Blue answered.

Despite the horrible nightmare they'd just left behind and the one they might still have to face at the hospital, it felt good to share this moment with Blue.

He kissed her.

Until he touched his mouth to hers, she hadn't realized just how much she needed it.

Needed *him*.

Rayanne didn't pull away from him when the kiss ended. She stayed there in his arms.

"You know I'm not going away when this is over, right?" he asked.

There was already too much buzzing through her head for her to try and think that through. Was he talking about moving closer to her, or was this about something else?

"What about your job?" she asked, because that was a lot safer than asking about that "something else."

He pointed to the Clay Ridge city-limits sign that was just ahead. "I can get reassigned here or else to Sweet-water Springs."

So they were talking about distance. Rayanne wasn't sure how she felt about that.

Okay, she was.

Yes, she wanted Blue closer. She wanted him to be a big part of their baby's life. But it terrified her to realize that she wanted more from him.

Blue's hand went to her stomach. "You just gasped again."

"Not because of the baby," she mumbled.

Blue stared at her, obviously waiting for her to explain that, but Rayanne had no idea how to even start.

"I'm in love with you, Blue," she blurted out.

That was it?

The best she could do?

Yes, her head was fuzzy, but judging from Blue's pole-axed look, she should have eased into it better. Or maybe she shouldn't have brought it—

He kissed her, cutting off the rest of that thought. In fact, it cut off a lot of things. Her fears. Doubts.

Common sense.

And for that moment, that one wonderful moment, Rayanne got totally wrapped up in his arms and in his kiss.

"Uh, I hate to interrupt," Colt said, "but we're at the hospital."

Oh, mercy. Yes, she was losing it, but the sight of the hospital brought it all home. Her mother could be inside there dying, and she had to focus on that and not the punch from one of Blue's kisses.

"We'll table the conversation for now," Blue said, still eyeing her with some emotion that she thought might be caution.

They got out of the car, and because the three of them were still on edge, they all put their hands over their weapons. Rayanne was more than a little relieved when she didn't see any need for concern.

Good thing, too, since there was more than enough concern in the waiting room.

The moment they stepped through the doors, a lanky dark-haired man wearing a badge approached them. "I'm Deputy Hawks from the Clay Ridge County sheriff's office."

Of course, she'd expected law enforcement to be there. And it wasn't just the deputy, either. She spotted a county jail guard she recognized from her visits to her mother.

"Is there any update on my mother?" Rayanne immediately asked.

Deputy Hawks shook his head. "She's still in surgery."

He motioned for them to follow him and took them into a smaller, private waiting room just up the hall. "Figured you'd be more comfortable in here."

Blue and Rayanne mumbled a thanks, and Colt stepped to the side of the room when he got another call.

The deputy took a seat near the door. "Sheriff Braddock's on the way to the scene of his grandfather's explosion. After that, he'll assist moving the prisoners to the jail over in Sweetwater Springs."

Good. She had enough on her plate without having to deal with another Braddock tonight. From all accounts, Sheriff Aiden Braddock was an upright peace officer, but she'd had her fill of Wendell and his entire family.

"You should sit," Blue said, and he tried to get her to do that, but her body didn't cooperate. She was suddenly too wired to do anything but pace.

Blue paced with her.

Now that she could actually see him, she looked him over to make sure he wasn't injured.

He was.

There were new scrapes and bruises on his face and hands. Probably on the rest of his body, too. That was when she realized she probably looked just as bad. She pushed her hair from her face, causing Blue to smile.

"You're beautiful," he said as if reading all the doubts in her mind.

She nearly pointed out that it was a lie, but Rayanne found herself smiling. Briefly, anyway. "Thanks."

"So, you're in love with me?" he asked.

Okay, here was where she could say it'd all been a mistake. Something she'd blurted out in the heat of the moment. Then things could go back to the way they were before.

But she didn't want that.

Rayanne nodded. "Sorry. I know that only complicates things."

He squinted one eye, gave her a funny look. "It could, I suppose. Especially if that means you'd add me to the list of people you'd take a bullet for."

It did indeed add him to the list. Except the list was sort of on hold right now because the baby had to come first.

"You won't take a bullet for me," he insisted. "But I appreciate the thought. I'd take a bullet for you, too."

That made her heart soar. And fall. "That list wasn't meant to be a nightmare come true," she insisted. "No more taking bullets."

Maybe that would include no more bullets being fired at them, too.

"No more," Blue mumbled.

Anything else he was about to add to that was cut off when Roy and Rosalie came rushing into the room. Rosalie ran to her, pulled her into her arms.

"Anything yet?" her sister asked.

But Rayanne had to shake her head. She let go of her sister so she could face Roy. There was way too much pain between them for her to pull him into a hug, but she was careful not to issue him her standard glare.

"Thank you," she mumbled. "For everything."

Roy nodded. Blinked hard as if blinking back tears and nodded again. "Glad I was there."

That made Rayanne have to blink hard, too.

Thankfully, Colt gave them a reprieve when he finished his call. "The deputy found Ruby-Lee," he relayed to them. "She was tied up at Wendell's house. Wendell told her his men would be there to take care of her once they finished with Rayanne and Blue."

Thank God those men were now in custody and couldn't harm her. Rayanne made a mental note to call the woman and thank her when this ordeal was over.

And once Blue and she had worked out the possible complications of her *I love you* and the near tears she'd just shed over Roy.

"Cooper got a look inside what was left of Wendell's car," Colt went on. "Two bodies. One of them was definitely Wendell."

So it was really over.

Well, the danger was, anyway.

But the damage to her family might have already been done, and the proof of that stepped into the doorway. Not a doctor but rather a nurse, according to her name tag.

"The doctor will be here in just a few minutes to give you an update," the woman said. "But I wondered if any of you have B-negative blood?"

Oh, God. That sounded serious. "Why?" Rayanne asked.

"It's the patient's type. We're running short, and we usually ask family to donate in situations like this." Her attention landed on Rayanne's stomach. "Can't take a donation from you, though. Nor you," she added, eyeing Blue's injuries.

"I'm O positive, anyway," Blue said.

Rayanne shook her head. "And I'm not B negative. I'm A positive."

Rosalie mumbled the same.

So did Roy.

"I'm B negative," Colt said, stepping ahead of them. He suddenly didn't look too pleased that he and his estranged mother shared the same blood.

Of course, Rayanne was no doubt looking similar about Roy's and her blood connection. It was strange how things worked out like that.

Colt followed the nurse, but he'd been gone only a few seconds when someone else stepped into the doorway.

Seth.

He made it to Rosalie and her in what seemed to be one giant step, and he pulled them both into his arms. "You're both hardheaded for trying to come here." But he brushed kisses on their foreheads and looked at Blue.

"How many thanks do I owe you for watching out for them?" Seth asked.

"None. No thanks necessary. I have my own pretty high stake in all of this." Blue put his hand over Rayanne's stomach. Then eased her back to him. No forehead kiss. He gave her one of his winners right on the mouth.

Seth smiled. Well, sort of. Her brother wasn't actually the smiling sort, but since he wasn't scowling, that was close enough.

Blue tipped his head to Roy. "But we both owe him some thanks. He helped get us out of there. Colt, too."

That caused Seth's usual scowl, but Seth softened— just a little—when he nodded, a gesture that appeared to be a thank-you. Whatever it was, no one had time to dwell on it, because the man in scrubs stepped into the room.

"I'm Dr. Dayton." And with just those few words, he

had everyone's attention. "I did Jewell's surgery to remove some shrapnel from her abdomen. Some of it was deeply embedded, and she lost a lot of blood, but no vital organs were hit. She'll be fine."

Rayanne hadn't even known she was holding her breath until her lungs started to ache. The relief was instant, her breath whooshing out, and she practically collapsed into Blue's waiting arms.

"I need to see her," Rayanne managed to say.

The doctor glanced at all of them. Finally nodded. Just when Rayanne thought she was going to have to get ugly and demand it.

"But keep it short," the doctor warned them, and he motioned for the family to follow him. He led them farther down the hall to the surgical-recovery suites.

Rayanne spotted another guard, a reminder that her mother would be returned to jail as soon as possible. She held her breath again when the doctor opened the door, and she got her first glimpse of her mother.

She was too pale, was Rayanne's first reaction. Too weak looking with all those machines hooked up to her.

But then Jewell opened her eyes and smiled. There was an IV in her arm, but she waggled her fingers, motioning for them to come closer.

They did. All of them. Including Roy. But he stayed back while Rosalie, Seth and she gave their mom gentle kisses on the cheek. The smile lingered on her mouth a little longer until she studied Blue's and Rayanne's fresh injuries.

"Who did this?" Jewell asked, but she turned her attention to Roy for an answer.

"Wendell." And that was all he said. All that needed to

be said. With just the man's name, her mother no doubt knew the motive.

Revenge.

"He's dead," Rayanne added. "He can't hurt us anymore."

Of course, the upcoming murder trial could. But Rayanne pushed that aside. For now, her mother was okay, and that was enough.

"Blue," Jewell said, motioning for him to come closer, too. Her grip seemed as fragile as fine crystal, but she caught on to his hand and pulled him down for a kiss on the cheek. "You'll take good care of Rayanne and my grandbaby."

"I will," Blue said without hesitation. "In fact, I was just about to ask Rayanne to marry me. Figured this was a good time and place to do it."

Rayanne choked on the gulp of air she sucked in. "This is the first I've heard about a proposal."

"Because you've missed a boatload of signals," Seth grumbled. "The guy's in love with you. I'm not sure why, but he is, so my advice is to say yes before the doctor boots us out of here."

"Are you?" Rayanne asked, sounding so stunned that it caused Blue to laugh.

Mercy, she loved that laugh, almost as much as she loved him.

Blue hooked his arm around her waist, pulled her closer. "Of course I'm in love with you. And I love our baby and the life we're going to have together." He paused to kiss her.

Oh, heck. It was one of those mind-scrambling kisses that robbed her of the ability to think. Not good. She figured this was a time when she needed all of her wits.

"Well, I will love our life together if you say yes," Blue amended.

Rayanne nearly glanced at Rosalie, Seth and her mom to see what their reactions were.

But then she realized it didn't matter.

Yes, she wanted them to approve. Wanted them to be happy for her, but she knew in her heart there was only one thing that would make her truly happy.

And he was standing right in front of her.

Rayanne didn't make him wait. "Yes."

Or at least, she got most of the word out before Blue kissed her again. Everything fell into place.

Rayanne pulled back, meeting her mother's gaze. Then she glanced around the rest of the room. This wasn't about rifts, the trial or injuries. It was about one thing.

Family.

Rayanne put her arms around the man she loved and pulled Blue to her for another kiss.

* * * * *

Next month, be sure to pick up the next book in
USA TODAY *bestselling author Delores Fossen's*
miniseries SWEETWATER RANCH.
You'll find KIDNAPPING IN KENDALL COUNTY
wherever Harlequin Intrigue books are sold!

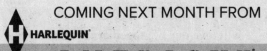

REQUEST YOUR FREE BOOKS!
2 FREE NOVELS PLUS 2 FREE GIFTS!

◆HARLEQUIN®
INTRIGUE®

BREATHTAKING ROMANTIC SUSPENSE

YES! Please send me 2 FREE Harlequin Intrigue® novels and my 2 FREE gifts (gifts are worth about $10). After receiving them, if I don't wish to receive any more books, I can return the shipping statement marked "cancel." If I don't cancel, I will receive 6 brand-new novels every month and be billed just $4.74 per book in the U.S. or $5.24 per book in Canada. That's a savings of at least 14% off the cover price! It's quite a bargain! Shipping and handling is just 50¢ per book in the U.S. and 75¢ per book in Canada.* I understand that accepting the 2 free books and gifts places me under no obligation to buy anything. I can always return a shipment and cancel at any time. Even if I never buy another book, the two free books and gifts are mine to keep forever.

182/382 HDN F42N

Name _____ (PLEASE PRINT)

Address _____ Apt. #

City _____ State/Prov. _____ Zip/Postal Code

Signature (if under 18, a parent or guardian must sign)

Mail to the **Harlequin® Reader Service:**
IN U.S.A.: P.O. Box 1867, Buffalo, NY 14240-1867
IN CANADA: P.O. Box 609, Fort Erie, Ontario L2A 5X3
Are you a subscriber to Harlequin Intrigue books
and want to receive the larger-print edition?
Call 1-800-873-8635 or visit www.ReaderService.com.

* Terms and prices subject to change without notice. Prices do not include applicable taxes. Sales tax applicable in N.Y. Canadian residents will be charged applicable taxes. Offer not valid in Quebec. This offer is limited to one order per household. Not valid for current subscribers to Harlequin Intrigue books. All orders subject to credit approval. Credit or debit balances in a customer's account(s) may be offset by any other outstanding balance owed by or to the customer. Please allow 4 to 6 weeks for delivery. Offer available while quantities last.

Your Privacy—The Harlequin® Reader Service is committed to protecting your privacy. Our Privacy Policy is available online at www.ReaderService.com or upon request from the Harlequin Reader Service.

We make a portion of our mailing list available to reputable third parties that offer products we believe may interest you. If you prefer that we not exchange your name with third parties, or if you wish to clarify or modify your communication preferences, please visit us at www.ReaderService.com/consumerchoice or write to us at Harlequin Reader Service Preference Service, P.O. Box 9062, Buffalo, NY 14269. Include your complete name and address.

HI13R

"Maybe you don't understand the fine line between snooping and jail. Breaking and entering is—"

"I'm going with you." Donning a hat and gloves, Gillian turned to look at him.

Austin was smiling at her as if amused.

"What?" she said, suddenly feeling uncomfortable under his scrutiny. She knew it was silly. He'd seen her at her absolute worst.

"You just look so…cute," he said. "Clearly, breaking the law excites you."

She smiled in spite of herself. It had been a while since a man had complimented her. But it wasn't breaking the law that excited her.

She breathed in the freezing air. It stung her lungs, but made her feel more alive than she had in years. Fear drove her steps along with hope.

At the dark alley, Austin slowed. It was late enough that there were lights on in the houses.

"Come on," Austin said, and they started to turn down the alley.

A vehicle came around the corner, moving slowly. Gillian felt the headlights wash over them, and she let out a worried sound as she froze in midstep.

Her moment of panic didn't subside when she saw that it was a sheriff's department vehicle.

"Austin?" she whispered, not sure what to do.

He turned to her and pulled her into his arms. Her mouth opened in surprise, and the next thing she knew, he was kissing her. At first, she was too stunned to react. But after a moment, she put her arms around his neck and lost herself in the kiss.

As the headlights of the sheriff's car washed over them, she let out a small helpless moan as Austin deepened the kiss, drawing her even closer.

The sheriff's car went on past, and she felt a pang of regret. Slowly, Austin drew back a little. His gaze locked with hers, and for a moment they stood like that, their quickened warm breaths coming out in white clouds.

"Sorry."

She shook her head. She wasn't sorry. She felt…light-headed, happy, as if helium-filled. She thought she might drift off into the night if he let go of her.

"Are you okay?" he asked, looking worried.

She touched the tip of her tongue to her lower lip. "Great. Never better."

Find out what happens next in
DELIVERANCE AT CARDWELL RANCH
by New York Times *bestselling author B.J. Daniels,*
available December 2014,
only from Harlequin Intrigue.